Looking for Mrs. Santa Claus

By

Margaret Carlyle Price

authorHOUSE™

1663 LIBERTY DRIVE, SUITE 200
BLOOMINGTON, INDIANA 47403
(800) 839-8640
WWW.AUTHORHOUSE.COM

First published by AuthorHouse 11/15/04

ISBN: 1-4184-9389-9 (sc)

Printed in the United States of America
Bloomington, Indiana

This book is printed on acid-free paper.

Looking for Mrs. Santa Claus is dedicated to my three daughters Meredith, Julie and Katie, whose Belief and letters to Santa inspired the story.

And to my husband, Gary Swim, whose Spirit personifies Christmas.

Thank you to Karen Karnezous who's artistic talents made the cover possible.

And to all wise and wonderful "reindeer" disguised as chocolate labs, golden retrievers and old greyhounds.

Dear Santa,
How did you meet your wife?

Love, caite

P.S. Do you have a dog?

P.S.S I always will believe in you

CHAPTER ONE

Somewhere, on a tropical paradise south of the North Pole ...

Shadows of coconut palm trees cast against a white sand beach, deserted except for a giant beach umbrella.

Waves splash. Seagulls honk, noisily.

Bing Crosby, sounding a little tinny and crackling thin, croons "White Christmas" out of a beach boom box. Then Bing disappears into the butter melting voice of Pippa McKenzie, announcing the Personals on the radio show "Lovin', Lookin' or Leavin' "--

"Sizzling Sugar Cookie in Sweetwater, Mississippi is looking for love. Must have own hair. No cats. Cute ears. Naughty sugar and spice, in NYC is looking for a Teddy Bear to tickle her pink."

Suddenly, the wind plays tricks. The beach umbrella tilts, rolls and somersaults up and over the most fantastic sandcastle imaginable. With towers and turrets. draw-bridge and moat. Decorated with seashells of every kind -- Angel wings and kitten paws, shark tooth and turkey wings. Kneeling down beside the castle is a diminutive figure in a broad brimmed straw bonnet. She grasps hold of the umbrella, and rises, spinning magically, sprinkling the castle with pearls of spilt sand. Higher and higher, she twirls. Her bare toes, painted rather curiously polka dot red and green, tickle the warm wind. She throws back her head, laughing. Then, she whistles.

It is the kind of whistle that only old dogs can hear. For it comes, not from human lips, but from the depth of the human soul.

I

And then, from out of the sea comes a flash of fur, shaking ferociously. Pounding wet sand, flying. An old, old greyhound, looking more like a chocolate chip cookie, rises slowly, majestically, racing the waves. Challenging the wind. Her great paws swim through the air, her wings (which are invisible) beat at an incredible speed. Up she flies, higher and higher, until she wrestles the umbrella out of the grip of the naughty wind, catches it in her teeth and gracefully drops it at the bare toes of the sand sculptor.

The sand artist scratches the dog between her ears. Grateful, the old greyhound flops over on her belly, tongue hanging sideways and shakes.

"Thank you."

Settling into a beach chair, the sand sulptor leans down, gathers wet sand, shaping it into a sleigh, then eight tiny reindeer and then, a greyhound which she places at the very lead. As Pippa continues with the Personals, ("Forty. Fat and Fabulous in Tucson, Arizona, seeks soul-mate to dance Hot Salsa and eat. Chocolate kisses an extra treat!") the old dog and sand sculptor gaze out over a seascape of Christmas sand sculptures--Candy Canes, a Bell and an Elf.

Pippa, sounding ever so perky, purrs-- "Lucky in love. Lucky in life. Well, that's it for our Personals on this balmy Christmas day eve. And for "Lovin', Lookin' or Leavin', I'm Pippa wishing you the love of your life and a very Merry Christmas.'

The boom box sizzles into static and then silence. The small sand sculptor opens a large carpet bag, takes out a lap-top and promptly types--

My dearest Caperton,
Bless you, honey. You found the perfect spot for
a little R& R. Really, you are quite the romantic elf.
Tell Santa to pack light and oh,
leave Blitzen up north. Much too hot for the
reindeer here.

As always, with love and
affection ...

2

"R-r--r!" A wet nose nudges the woman's hand. She pauses, looking up.

A star appears on the horizon.

The greyhound places his huge head in the woman's lap. They sit still, listening to the silence. Letting it whisper to their hearts.

Then, she remembers what she almost forgot. And adds a postscript.

"Oh and Cape,
If it's not too late, I noticed a little girl down here
who is in need of a pair of shoes (flip flops, polka
dot pink and yellow) and who is desperate
for a kitten. I was thinking of that white
and black kitten, the one who looks like he's
wearing a tuxedo. Sprinkle some of Santa's
magical Christmas Sugar and Spice and Everything
Nice on the tip of his ears and turn him from
stuffed into a real life kitten. The child's name
is Charlotte Elizabeth and she lives just behind
the row of palm trees by the pier."

With a peppermint kiss,
always-- Mrs. Claus

She hits a key on the lap-top, expecting to zing off the e-mail.

Nothing happens. The dog whines. Mrs. Claus hits a different key. She tries again. And again. The dog's paws shoot to her ears; her tail hits hard against dusty sand.

Then suddenly the screen goes blank. The lap-top sings "We wish you a Merry Christmas and shuts off. And seemingly undaunted, the woman simply and quietly folds her hands, closes her eyes and takes a very deep breath. She sneaks a peek at the greyhound, "Oh come on, if Cape can do it. So can we. Just feel what it would be like . . . ah!"

The greyhound sneezes, "Ah-ah-choo!"

The woman wiggles her bare toes in the sand, "Not that kind of 'ah'. Ah-ah-ah! Ancient wisdom of the elves!" The greyhound sneezes again. And again.

"Bless you, honey. You're not coming down with a cold?" She looks deep into the dog's eyes. She winks. "Yes, of course, it all began with a sneeze." I'd almost forgotten ..." She quietly takes the starfish christening the sandcastle and tosses it to a seagull. The gull spreads wide his wings, holding the Starfish firmly in his orange beak and flies out over the Gulf.

"I'd almost forgotten, last Christmas, Santa had a cold."

CHAPTER TWO

Whiteness swirls magically into giant snowflakes which then materialize into bubbles holding miniature candy canes inside. They bounce and float on an icy wind, toppling just above the reach of an elf, Cape, who is desperately trying to capture the naughty bubbles and tuck them back inside a large Candy Cane Bubble Blower.

Suddenly, a loud sneeze startles the befuzzle out of the elf and the bubbles burst with the tiny candy canes melting into something a' bit like cotton candy which then disappears as soon as it lands on the hard, frozen ground. The Christmas village is very still; all the elves, if elves there be in this place, are tucked in bed or sipping their chicken noodle soup. For it is Christmas day--but not a very cheery one.

Santa Claus has a cold.

A very bad, nasty cold. And a cough. And his voice is hoarse.

Cape, obedient elf that he is, trails after the sneezing Santa, straight into the Candy Cane Castle. Santa trails melting snow and soot across the cobblestone floor. A giant Christmas tree rises above a room in complete disarray with spilt cocoa, half-munched cookies and gooey marshmallows stuck to unwashed plates. Toy airplanes with missing wings, dolls with mixed-up shoes, stuffed bears with bunny ears all lie about the room as if dropped there by elves in great haste. It is all quite a mess.

Santa, weary, rumpled and red-nosed, slumps down into a chair; he looks in his pocket and the very last second, finds his handkerchief and blows his nose. He wrings out his handkerchief and coughs. "Ah-ah-chew! Cape!" Santa yawns in the middle of the sneeze, points towards his boots. "My, uh oh," (an even bigger sneeze!) boots!"

Cape, wearing an emerald green and purple cape, wipes up the snow, gathers up the toys. His spirit is undaunted. He will keep Christmas in his little elfin heart--yes, he will. He kneels down in front of Santa and pulls off the not-so-jolly Elf's boots. This is not an easy trick for the little elf, but good-naturedly, he pants, "It was another good year, sir."

Santa points to his throat, "Can't, can't talk." He sneezes.

Cape scampers over to a fireplace, pokes at some embers--glances around to see if Santa's watching and quickly throws some magic dust into the fire; flames leap and zing and give a lovely warm glow to the biting chill. The elf wiggles his nose and causes the fire to burn bright colors--tinsel silver and amber gold. It's quite a fireworks show--but lost on Santa who is blowing his nose.

Cape picks up old cups, "May I get you something hot, sir. Perhaps some peppermint tea? Or a latte? Some Chai with just a dash of nutmeg? No." The elf keeps talking although Santa keeps sneezing. "Or a cup of hot cocoa? With frothy whipped cream, dash of cinnamon sprinkle, a little bit of chocolate shavings, topped off with some delicious dark chocolate shaped into a stocking!? That'll do the trick."

Cape rummages through sticky cups and saucers, trying to find a clean cup in the cupboard. He gives up and sets about washing a cup with gooey gum. "Or what about some green tea? Terrific stuff, sir. I was watching Oprah just the other day, oh not really watching--listening, sir, while I was wrapping some of the Alexander dolls for the little girl in . . .well, never mind, there was a guest on the show who said . . . let's see, something about Green Tea having polythenols. Same as in dark chocolate. Good for catching the light in your jolly fat belly. Oh not that you're fat, sir. No. Nothing like that. Pleasantly plump, that's what I always say to the reindeer. Not that the reindeer and I were talking about you--being fat or anything. Ah, Green Tea melts the belly. Now coffee stores fat in the belly--but not tea. Why the North Pole should become a Kingdom of Green

Tea drinkers. And chocolate. Heavenly reindeer, haven't I always believed chocolate, dark, rich, delicious chocolate could fix a cold."

Cape chatters on, merrily stirring up a scrumptious brew of hot cocoa, shaving in dark chocolate. He whistles, blowing on the pot, "Be just a second, sir. Just waiting for the pot to sing." He whistles, merrily. He's trying awfully hard to capture the Christmas spirit which seems to be escaping with every sneeze--straight out the chimney.

"Cape?" Santa stirs, loosening his belt.

"Sir, got 'er right here. Chocolate green tea." He pours some of the green elixir into a mug and offers it to Santa.

"No, thanks." He sneezes. Louder (if that's possible!) You'll see to the ..." (a cough, sneeze and yawn all in one breath!!) reindeer?" Santa closes his eyes.

Cape sighs, sniffs the steam coming off the drink. He takes a tiny sip. He dips a chocolate kiss into the mixture, smiles. Licks his fingers which are slender, and tapered and glow, whitish on the tips. He puts down the cup, nods and heads towards the door.

"Cape?"

Santa's voice catches the elf by surprise. Thrilled, Cape turns, quickly picking up the cup of Cheer. "Yes." Cape is all ears.

"Oh, oh ..." Santa sneezes.

"Was there something else, Santa?"

"Would you sit with me for awhile." Santa's voice sounds raspy and tired. Cape instantly pulls up a stool near the fire and turns to Santa who leans forward, as if about to confide a deep secret.

"Caperton, do you", he drops his voice to a whisper as if afraid someone might hear but the truth is, there is no one to hear-- except the forgotten toys and the Christmas tree-- "do you ever feel lonely?"

"There's always a' bit of a let down, isn't there, sir? After all the rushing and wrapping and unwrapping, the eating and drinking ... ah let me be of service, sir." Cape goes up on tip-toe and practically pirouettes over to the hearth where he begins madly grating chocolate into bubbling milk on a pot swinging over the fire. Steam wafts up into puffs shaped like miniature Caperton elves. He wiggles his ears and changes the puffs to tiny cups of cocoa and then into

7

chocolate hearts, wrapped in gold foil, which circle Santa. Oblivious to the magic trying to burst in upon his cold, Santa takes a shallow breath, looking even more exhausted. He raises an eyebrow, glancing at Cape--

"You're a good elf, Caperton. I couldn't do Christmas without you. Without all of you and the reindeer. Be sure and thank Rudolph. Such a noble fellow. Getting a tad far-sighted but . . ." His words disappear into a yawn.

Cape pours the hot cocoa into a cup, "Ah why mess with a good thing. Hot cocoa, plain and simple. Save the Green Tea for the Rabbit." Here you go, Santa." He turns to offer the cocoa to Santa, "Your cocoa, sir?"

Santa is snoring.

Cape puts down the cup. He pulls a blanket up over Santa, "Oh well, later. Sweet dreams, sir. Sweet dreams." Cape tip-toes out of the room, closing the door behind him.

CHAPTER THREE

Once outside, Cape's ears shoot up. Music blares across the village. The elf glances towards the stables where he catches a glimpse of a reindeer flying upside down. He takes off across the crunching snow, heading towards a boom box propped up on a fence post just outside the stables.

An elf, with an earring in his nose, curly hair slightly spiked and highlighted orange, gyrates to the music. He's flipping through the burlap bag, spilled open inside Santa's sleigh. "Yuck, peanut butter." The elf takes a bite and tosses it. Then another. And another. "Yo, Blitzen, dude." He pulls out a carrot. "Lucky you, it's the only thing in the bag that won't take a bite out of you." He tosses the carrot to the reindeer.

But, the reindeer ducks and the carrot hits Cape smack between his big ears, which are really twitching.

"Christmas Jingles, you hit my ear." Cape turns down the music.

"What's the matter bro, you don't like Motown?" Jingles takes another bite. "Yuck. Stale." He keeps at it—nibbling cookies, "Mushy. Gooey. Raspberry. Yo, Cape, there hasn't been a decent cookie since Easy Bake Oven."

Cape bites into a small jam cake shaped like a bell.

"Hey, Jingles, try this. Some kind of jam cake, caramel icing--you'll like it."

"Creative but I'm looking for something chocolate."

A loud sneeze coming from the castle splits the snowflakes into a thousand twinkling bits of ice that duck for cover beneath the reindeer's antlers. The reindeer stare at the castle, then retreat (all but Blitzen) back inside the stables. Another sneeze and the headset flies off Jingle's ears, getting tangled in Blitzen's antlers.

"Jumping jelly beans, this one's worse than last year."

Cape untangles the headset.

"And his nose, did you get a look at that. He could get Rudolph's job."

From inside the stables, there's the sound of a loud reindeer snort. Jingles glances over his shoulder, "Sorry, Rudolph."

"He's just a little under the weather, Jingles.,"

"Under the weather. Are you kidding, Cape. I'd say he's over an avalanche." Jingles turns up the radio. But instead of the Motown, a woman's voice, silky smooth and sweet as French Vanilla ice cream, rises over the fits of distant sneezing.

"This is Pippa for "Lovin', Lookin' or Leavin'. We've got a Rose Dawn in Rome, Georgia looking for a man to toast her marshmallows. Rosie, this song's for you." Pippa's voice fades into "Sugar Pie Honey Bunch."

Jingles breaks into a smooth move, and climbs back up into the sleigh where he keeps checking out the bag. Cape perches up on the back rail, and takes out a handful of green pistachios.

"I'll make him some soup, Jingles."

From inside the burlap bag, Jingles moves gingerly through the baked goods, "What's with you and soup. You ask me, it's the same soup warmed over. Year after year. Soup bowl after soup bowl. Cracker crumb after ..."

Blitzen quietly trots over and turns up the radio. Pippa purrs- "Well, that's it for our personals. Listen to your heart and let me hear from ya'll. Call or send me an e-mail at Pippawww.com."

Jingles' head pops out of the bag. He is all ears. "That's it, Cape."

"You got a good cookie?" Cape cracks a pistachio and tosses it to Blitz.

"I got a great cookie! Look, Cape, you and the Big Guy, you're like best friends. Elf to elf. Do anything for him?"

"Let me see that cookie, Jingles?" Cape reaches for the cookie in Jingles' hand.

"I'm not talking cookies. I'm talking Cookies. Candy. Sugar pie. Honey. And everything nice." Jingles does a back flip and does an Elvis twist with his hips, singing, "Sugar pie honey bunch." "He improvises, "Sugar, ooh-oooh, Ooh sugar, sugar. you are my candy, babe. And you got me running. Sugar. Ooh-ooh. Oh, sugar, sugar."

Blitzen rolls his eyes.

"Give me that cookie." Cape tosses the cookie to Blitz who eyes it suspiciously.

"I'm not talking cookies. I'm talking a Sugar Cookie as in "Lovin', Lookin' or Leavin'. As in a babe for Saint Nick. As in looking for a Mrs. Santa Claus."

"You're kidding, right, Jingles."

Jingles grins.

"You're not kidding."

Jingles is way ahead of Cape. He puts his arm around the reindeer, drawing him in. "Hey Blitz, help me out here, would you? Work with me. You got a way with words."

Blitzen blinks. Thinking. He whispers a possible phrase into Jingles' big ears.

"Not bad. Not bad, Blitz. Jolly old elf seeks . . . wait, let me write this down. You got a pen?" Blitzen trots over to a board with messages like "Feed Donner twice a day. Extra oats for Rudolph." He bites off the black felt pen and slips it into Jingles' palm.

"Great. Here, turn around, Cape."

Cape turns around. Jingles writes on the back of the elf's t-shirt.

"Cut it out, Jingles, that tickles."

"Hold still. Now, here we go. Something like- 'Jolly old elf seeks pretty lady to . . .

Blitzen whispers some more words into Jingles' ears.

" . . . Right. Great. . . . to spend eternity making kids Christmas wishes come true."

Blitzen swishes his tail in Jingles' face.

"Oh yeah, all right. Something about soup. . . . seeks lady who cooks great chicken noodle soup to spend eternity. . . This is good. This is really good. Got it."

Cape tries to look at his back, wiggles his nose. He's getting suspicious. "Shouldn't we ask the 'big guy'?

"What? And spill the beans on the best Christmas present ever? No way. Think Christmas. Think Secrets. Think Mistletoe!"

Jingles takes a palm computer out of his pocket. He opens it and types, "Okay, here she goes. Pippawww.com. "Jolly old elk, oops, elf .. . where's the Spelling, under Tools, okay . . . lets' see, . . . 'elf (he keeps typing) . . . seeks pretty lady who cooks' (and he starts humming) 'tasty chicken noodle soup to spend eternity . . .'"

He finishes the personal and hands the computer to Cape.

Cape stares at the computer. Jingles shows him the e-mail button. "Here, Cape. Zing it."

Cape closes his eyes. Opens them. "I don't know, Jingles. I don't feel quite right about this."

"What's feeling have to do with this. This is a matter of doing the right thing. Forget feeling. Just do it."

Cape places his finger close to the button; there's a slight whitish glow about the tip of his finger-- he whispers, "For the good of all, especially children. At the right time, the right place, under divine guidance . . ."

Jingles presses his hand down over Cape's finger and hits the send button. There is a loud buzz. Cape's ears twitch, "Light speed."

The computer glistens.

Cape opens his eyes, "Now what?"

"Well, like the Great Elf said, 'The rest is destiny.'

As the computer glows brighter, it becomes rather hot. Cape hands it back to Jingles who gathers up some snowflakes to cool the energy field.

"What Great Elf?" Cape licks a snowflake off his hand.

"You're lookin' at him."

Suddenly, Cape makes a wild dive, trying to seize the computer, "Jingles! Jingles! Give me back that . . ."

"It's too late. Too late. Destiny is dancing with fate. 'Lovin', Lookin' or Leavin' has it that Santa Claus is looking for a play-mate."

Jingles breaks into a Motown Medley with the reindeer singing back-up. "Ooh, I feel good. You know that I do, girl. So good. So good. I got you, babe."

Cape gazes at his palms, emitting a white light. As he moves them in a circular motion, the light dances. He breathes deeply, then, folds his hands over his heart and whispers, "For the good of all."

A loud sneeze drowns out Motown. Jingles glances at Cape, "I kind'a wish we'd changed that part about soup to cookies. What do you think?"

Another sneeze. And this time, when Jingles looks up, Cape has disappeared. Leaving behind, a trail of pistachios that glisten in the coming of dusk light.

CHAPTER FOUR

Bubbles float down out of a Banyan Tree. It's the biggest Banyan Tree in southwest Florida. Maybe in the universe. It looks like a giant walking elephant with a parasol. Roots shoot down into a cracked sidewalk. Paper palm fronds feather out over branches that curl and twist up and up and up--magically. There's something wonderful and mysterious about this tree. And it's not just the bubbles. Or the bare feet sticking out from over a branch. It has to do with the way the tree catches the light and casts shadows on the cool pavement below.

The Banyan Tree knows secrets.

Across the street, a canary yellow Cottage stands on crooked stairs, leaning against the wind towards the distant Gulf (which is visible at the far end of the street.) A second floor window suddenly flies open and a woman's head pops out between white muslin curtains. This is Dee; she's thirty-something, pretty and pretty over-whelmed by laundry and packing boxes, laundry and washing dishes, laundry and chasing errant hamsters. She leans out over the windowsill--

"Chelsea Rose! Chelsea Rose!"

A small voice speaks from the Banyan Tree, "Princess Aurora."

"The Agency is sending someone over. Ups ..." She stops mid-sentence, deciding to spell the name, "U--p--s ..." but her voice is drowned out by a UPS truck spitting gravel, screeching tires as it kicks dust and turns up the quiet street.

"Ma'am?" Chelsea Rose glances up through papaya green leaves, eyeing the wisp of curtain that has floated down over her mother's head.

Dee emerges from the fallen curtain and glances at the driver of the UPS truck; she pulls the curtain up around her, as if conscious that she wasn't properly attired for shouting out the window at her little girl. She waves to the UPS driver, "Chelsea, I'm just going to pop into the little girl's room."

The UPS man looks up and waves, rather surprised, at Dee. He starts up the walk, towards the Banyan Tree. A bubble hits him in the face. He looks up and sees painted toes wiggling out of the tree.

"Hello, Princess."

"Do I know you? I don't think I know you." Chelsea Rose's blonde head pops out of the branches; she's wearing a crown.

"UPS, 'Guaranteed to Please.'" He tips his cap. "I'm looking for Number 5 Peppermint Palm." He pops a bubble, starts towards an arbor/gate around the side of the tree.

"Oh, UPS. Nobody lives back there. Except for the black snake." Chelsea Rose stirs the bubble juice and waves the wand, splashing the hot, still air with tiny bubbles which she pops with her toes. Her words definitely get the attention of the UPS driver; he stops. Turns and retreats.

"Number 5's across the street. That's my house."

"Oh yeah?" He glances at his note pad.

"Yep. They got the numbers mixed up when they painted the street. Would you like to play with me?"

Chelsea Rose, dressed up as a princess, or at least in a costume that might at one time have been the costume of a princess, blows a string of pear-like bubbles down onto the UPS man's balding head. He grins, looking up--

"I'd like that, princess, but I've got a package for your mother, the Queen. Aren't you a little high? Should you be up there all alone?"

"Oh, I'm not alone. Baby Ghost is with me." Chelsea climbs down onto a lower branch, curls her legs around the branch and scoots closer to the UPS driver. He backs up, staring at the wand which is waving bubbles. Suddenly she somersaults and giggles, swinging upside down.

"So, uh, what do you and Baby Ghost do up there in that tree?"

Chelsea swings right side up. "We look for fairies. Sometimes we find things. Like strawberries or carrot cake cupcakes. Once, we found a little jam cake in the shape of a bell. And yesterday, there was a whole key lime pie. Want to come up. See what you'll find?"

"I'd sure love to, princess, but another time. I'll bet that tree's fresh out of pies."

"I -- I don't think so." She holds out her hand; he helps her down. She pushes white-blonde bangs out of her eyes; they are blue, and speak of a wonder and innocence and grace belonging to those who climb Banyan Trees with imaginary friends like a Baby Ghost. The UPS driver glances at her dress, torn at the hem, dirty and drooping at the neck. He lets out a soft whistle, "What a beautiful costume."

"Oh, it's not a costume. I wear this every day." She waves a Princess Beach Bag over one bare shoulder and reaches into it for a pair of plastic princess shoes; one is green, the other pink. Unmatching except in their gold emblem. She ties up the bag, bulging with apples, strawberries, pieces of gold ribbon and a pie.

"Well, I'll be Jimmy Cricketted." He steps back and stares up into the twisted labyrinth of branches, "Could a'fooled me. It looks just like an ordinary old Banyan Tree."

Chelsea slips her small hand into his hand and whispers, "Well, you know, Mr. U.P.S., things aren't always what they look like." They start across the street; she suddenly turns, "Oh, we forgot Baby Ghost." She runs back to the Banyan Tree and holds out her arms to her make-believe friend-- "Just jump."

Then, satisfied that her friend is now with them, Chelsea Rose skips ahead of the UPS driver, laughing, "My mom's inside. She said for me to be on the lookout for you. Come on in. If you'd like, I'll let you marry Baby Ghost. But just for a little while."

"Well, thanks, princess. But all I need is a signature. Is the last name .. ?" He tries reading the scribbled name. "Swain?"

Chelsea giggles, "Uh-uh. Swan. Like the Ugly Duckling. My mom's expecting you. She's expecting a' lot of things; like a miracle, a maid, a cook ... a baby. I'll get her."

They walk up the sidewalk to the yellow clapboard house. Number 5 Peppermint Palm is painted on the front porch. Bougainvillea trail over the railing which is, like the plant, a tad parched and peeling. As Chelsea opens the screen door, Christmas music blares from a boom box inside.

"Mama, it's Mr. U.P.S. or whatever." She looks up into the kind face of the UPS driver and winks. "Don't be shy."

"Oh, I'll just wait ..."

Chelsea takes his hand, "Oh don't be silly. She's expecting a baby but you can't catch that. I don't think. Unless you drink the water. She's in here."

The UPS driver steps into the front room. It's not a house. It's a toy store. There are boxes everywhere--cereal boxes, moving boxes, boxes turned upside down into forts and fairy castles, spilling tiny puffy white balls. Real grown-up furniture is sparse--there's a TV. and a couch; but the couch has a dog lying on it. The dog resembles a fringed rug; he has a Christmas scarf tied around his head.

"That's Bo. The mailman brought him last Christmas; he's deaf." She places her princess beach bag on top of a lap-top computer in a leather case, takes a candy cane off a tilting Christmas tree and offers it, first to Baby Ghost (who evidently refuses) and then to the UPS driver.

"You're different from the others." Chelsea licks the candy cane, smiling.

The UPS driver glances around the room, a little nervous, "Are you sure your mother ...what others?"

Chelsea leads the nice UPS driver around a corner into a hall lined with children's drawings (of alligators and hamsters, of dragons and fairies). She skips ahead-- "She's back here. It's okay. We're leaving again in a couple of weeks. As soon as mom finds a house. But we can't find Chocolate Chip. I hope Bo didn't eat him."

The UPS driver follows, reluctantly, stepping around boxes. He eyes an empty hamster cage. About this time, the rug, Bo, who is actually a handsome brown and white feathered Springer Spaniel, springs off the couch and begins sniffing the man's ankles. This makes the UPS driver even more nervous; he catches up with Chelsea Rose just as she climbs over a box and pushes open a door into a bathroom.

"She's in here. She's always in here." Chelsea puts her fingers in her mouth, mimicking someone about to toss their cookies. As the door swings open, the UPS driver says,

"Uh, Mrs. Swain? I have a delivery ..."

Dee Swan is sitting on the potty; reading "My Upmost for His Highest." She looks up. "Oh, hello." Her voice actually sounds normal, cheerful.

The UPS driver covers his eyes; he holds out the signature pad.

Dee takes the pad, smiling, resigned to rising to the occasion, resigned to giving her "utmost for His highest" in any situation, "Do you have a pen?"

He opens one eye; takes a pen out of his pocket. Dee signs.

From the front of the house, a door opens, then slams shut. And a voice, sounding more like a war-cry, resonates against the uncarpeted floorboards, "Dee! Dee, where are you? He missed the damn free-throw. Fouled out. Dee!" There's the sound of something hitting hard against a wall and feathers flash by as a Macaw makes a sudden dive down the hall towards the bathroom. The UPS driver not only ducks, he too dives--back down the hall.

Chelsea Rose follows him, "You're not Upsky from the We Care About Kids Baby-sitting Agency?" She sounds disappointed.

He shakes his head; trying to step around Bo who is trailing, sniffing the guy's hands. The UPS driver finally takes a piece of horehound candy out of his pocket and tosses it to the dog, "That dog's got a great nose."

"Oh yes, he once ate a bar of soap. He'll eat anything." They reach the front door. "No wonder you're so nice."

"Chin up, princess. I'll bet something wonderful is waiting for you, just around the corner of that Banyan Tree."

She lights up and takes off singing, arms linked with Baby Ghost. Bo trails Chelsea, trying hard to dissolve the horehound candy. They disappear into the back of the house, leaving the UPS driver face to face with Warfield Swan.

"Oh hello!" The UPS driver sticks out his hand; Warfield, a charming, personable, robust and very short man in his mid-thirties. Warfield is peeling a banana, wheeling and dealing on two cell phones at the same time while also glaring at a small, curly headed boy. The boy, about eight, bounces a basketball against the kitchen wall. Warfield acknowledges the UPS driver with a grin, cocking his head-- since both hands are tied up between holding the cell phones and peeling the banana.

The UPS driver, a shade closer to ripe watermelon rather than raspberry peach, blushes and makes for the door. Warfield talks into the phone on his left ear, "We can do that. No problem." Then, he switches to the phone perched on his right shoulder and in a perfectly calm voice that has not the slightest hint of all the chaos whirling about his feet (a bouncing ball, a shirking kid, a choking dog), says-- "Hello, yeah, Graham, I'm all over it. No, can you, would you mind holding?" He pops the banana in his mouth.

Not only is Warfield Swan ambidextrous with his hands, but also with his ears. He's like a weasel, switching back and forth, oozing intelligence, a commander in chief on the battlefield of closing a Wal-mart deal. Unimpressed by his father's prowess, however, is Chad, dressed in basketball shorts, slouching towards the bathroom.

Warfield puts both phones on hold and trots after his slinking son. "Get back here, Chad. I'm not finished talking to you."

Chad flips him the bird, "Talk to the hand." and slams the bathroom door behind him. Seconds later, Dee emerges out of the same bathroom, brushing her teeth. Her hair is up in curlers.

Between her upper teeth and her bottom teeth, Dee manages to push her blonde hair back from her eyes, "Warfield, lower your voice. The whole neighborhood can hear you." She heads for the kitchen sink and finishes brushing.

Warfield follows her, "What neighborhood? We live next door to a Banyan Tree."

From outside, a loud honking rises above the Christmas music and the reverberating zing of a basketball bouncing off the bathroom floor. Dee glances out the window above the sink-- "Warfield, is the taxi here?" And of course, both of Warfield's cell phones play the opening line of "The National Anthem" and "We Wish You a Merry Christmas".

Warfield picks-up, "Hello. Can you hold? Great. "Hello, hey Goose, old buddy, how's ..."

Suddenly, the bouncing basketball slams against the kitchen screen door with a sullen Chad, red-faced and red-nosed, trailing close behind. Dee catches the ball, hands it to her son, "Sorry, honey. You missed the shot, huh? Have you seen Josh?"

Warfield tries to "close the deal", ushering Dee out of the kitchen. Dee follows Chad out into the hall. She takes hot curlers out of her hair, "Chad? Honey, don't walk away."

Chad looks like he's going to explode with anger. "Dad yelled so loud--I missed a free-throw and he just lost it. So, I shot him the finger and he, mom, you're not going to believe this ..."

Dee sighs, "Oh, I'll believe it." She puts the rollers on a cardboard box, which hisses from the heat.

"He pushed his way into the locker room. Trying to punch me. Coach had to get two guys to get him out of there."

"Chad, calm down. Lets' all just calm way down. Your dad's under a'lot of pressure right now. As soon as we move he closes the Wal-Mart deal, it's going to be different. He doesn't sleep; you know he's got this snoring thing ..."She makes a sound not unlike the sound the dog Bo is making, trying to dislodge the horehound candy from his throat. Dee glances at the dog and catches on that he's choking; she tries to give Bo the Heimlich maneuver but the dog's too fat. Finally, he just rolls over and burps.

Chad throws a pillow on the floor and starts up the stairs--"Right. Coach Kane had to get him out of the locker room. He hit me in the nose."

Warfield emerges from the kitchen, covering the left cell phone with his hand, "I didn't hit him. Kid's so big and clumsy, he tripped over his shoe-strings." He switches voices, melting sugar into the phone, "Oh yeah, I'm still here. You say when, where, how high, we're all over it."

Dee takes a candy cane off the tree and offers it to Chad, still lurking on the stairs, "Here, Chad. Calm down. Tie your shoelaces."

Chad bounces the ball against the stairs, "I'm too old for candy canes, mom." He takes off, kicking his shoes back down the stairs. They land with a heavy thud, just missing Bo.

Warfield puts one cell phone into his pocket; he walks over to a suitcase, lying half-open near the front door and begins rummaging through shirts, jockey-shorts-- "Dee, where are my black socks?"

Dee shoots the dog a look, "I don't know, Warfield. Try your feet." She takes a lick of the candy cane, starts to sit down on the stairs, then gets up and picks up Chad's shoes, "Hey guys, where's Josh?" This is spoken to no one in particular; she opens the front door-- "Oh my gosh, Warfield, the taxi's here."

Dee hurriedly brushes her fingers through her hair and sits down on top of a suitcase; "Where's Chelsea?"

CHAPTER FIVE

Dee drags the bulging suitcase out the door onto the porch. She stops, takes a couple of breaths and waves to Chelsea who is having a Tea Party under the Banyan Tree. "Hi sweetheart. Hi Baby Ghost."

Chelsea blows her a kiss. Dee drags the suitcase down the porch steps, towards the honking taxi. The suitcase, bulging at the seams, bounces against the last step and springs open. Dee immediately sits down on the suitcase, closing it. She struggles to her feet, calling behind her, "Warfield! The taxi!"

A boy, about ten, with shaggy brownish-blonde hair, rides up into the sandy yard, tilts his bike up against the porch and takes the suitcase-- "Mom, where's dad?"

Dee smiles, "Looking for his black socks."

"Did he check the poop in the back yard." They both break out laughing. Dee holds out her hand to her son and he pulls her up. Together, they pick up the lingerie, cotton dresses and t-shirts that have spilled out of the suitcase.

"Thanks, Josh." Dee looks at her oldest son, into his eyes which glaze over from her stare; he is a child with secrets. "Josh, look out for Chelsea while we're gone. It's almost Christmas and . . ."

"Sure." He interrupts, not wanting to be talked to as a child.

"She's still little and still believes."

"I know." His hands find his jacket pocket; he stuffs them deep into the folds, finds the yo-yo and tosses out a Walk-the -Dog. But there is something in his voice, a catch in the usual casualness, that

22

causes Dee to look up from re-packing the suitcase. She waves to the taxi, "Just one minute." She takes a moment, brushes sand off the porch steps and sits down, "Come here, let me look at you."

Hesitant, he sits down beside her, tossing out the yo-yo, catching it. Throwing it out again.

"Do you . . ." Dee brushes his hair out of his light eyes.

"What?"

"Do you believe?"

"What? In Santa Claus?"

Dee takes the half-licked candy cane out of her pocket and cracks it in two, offering some to Josh. He takes the candy. They sit, side-by-side, silently. Listening to the soft thud of the yo-yo, yawning out, coming home. Like a wave, smooth and calm, cresting towards the shore. "No." She answers her own thought. "Did you ever believe, Josh?"

He catches the yo-yo, holds it in his hands, cupped like something sacred. "No, not really."

She takes his hand; then, playfully tosses out the yo-yo and does a trick. "I wonder if I've made you grow up too soon. Your dad was always off, closing a deal somewhere. And you were always so, I don't know. So grown-up. I could talk to you. Then, Chad came and Chelsea Rose. Did you ever have a chance to be a kid?"

"Mom."

The taxi horn stings the stolen moment. Chelsea Rose gives a squeal. And holds her hands over the ears of Baby Ghost. But Josh keeps talking; wanting to make his mom feel okay about his lost childhood." I always believed in the Easter Rabbit."

"Really? You know what, so do I?" She squeezes his hand; then stands. When he opens his hand, he sees several dollar bills. "Just pocket change. You know, for a hamburger with the guys."

He does a curious thing with his forehead, sort of a boyish scowl, "What guys?"

"Well, take Chelsea and Baby Ghost out for some ice cream over at Tony's Off Third. They're putting up the tree. I think the Festival of Lights is Monday, or Tuesday."

The taxi horn has now taken on a life of its own. It's pulsing with the rising fury of one very impatient, irate taxi driver. Dee scoops

Josh up in her arms, which embarrasses him--then she starts towards the taxi, rolling the suitcase along the uneven sidewalk; it hits a crack and for a second goes air-borne, but lands, safe enough.

"I'll call you as soon as we get in the hotel in Kansas City. The Agency is sending out a Mrs. Upsky or Upslovsky. A Russian." She's almost to the taxi, smiling at the driver who is not smiling back--fortunately, he's swearing in a language that's not English.

From inside the Cottage, language that is English, festers and hisses, rising above the Christmas "tra-la-las", and "In Excelsior deo". Josh glances at his mom, "What's with dad?"

"Chad lost the basketball game. He hasn't got Wal-Mart yet. He can't find his black sock." Dee is almost to the taxi when a woman, in a black overcoat, in curlers, gets off the Naples Trolley. She looks like a giant winged bat, smoking cigarettes as she groans, heaving a large plastic purple purse, waving at Dee.

Dee, however, is doing her best to smile amicably at the taxi driver as she moves the bag into the back seat. She talks to Josh in a calm voice, "Your dad and I are staying . . ." She stops mid-sentence, seeing the woman slithering straight towards her son. "Oh, good, that must be Mrs. Upsky. The lady from the We Care About Kids Baby-sitter's Agency."

The taxi driver leans against the horn and suddenly, finds his English dictionary and sputters, "Lady, it is Christmas. I got lots of deliveries, you know? Yes?" He pecks his wristwatch; peck, peck. Josh glances from the pecking taxi driver to the winged Russian. There is something very bird-like about both the driver and the Russian.

Josh stares at the robust Russian walking towards him; she walks with her small head leading, or rather dragging her enormous body which sways and bobbles behind her. The coat sways out, covering whatever surprises might be concealed beneath her wings.

She stops, panting; grinds out the cigarette.

Dee smiles, whispering, "Try and like this one. Well, I don't care if you like her but don't let Chad lock her in the basement. Or pour honey in her hair. Or shoot her with his beebee gun."

Warfield appears, banging shut the screen door. It sings, drops off one hinge. Warfield is oblivious to the sinking door. "Lets' go. Dee. Go. Go." His phone rings. The National Anthem plays.

24

Bo makes like a wild Angus bull, heading straight toward the Russian, dragging his leash. Dee grabs for the leash. Bo wags his tail and lifts his leg on the large Russian baby-sitter. She sputters. "Your, your dog . . ."

Bo circles; the black-raincoat baby-sitter circles.

"Oh oh. No. Go. Go."

The dog sprays her.

She hits at him with her umbrella. "Go. Go."

The dog turns on his heels and scuffs up grass. Dee grabs for the leash; Bo runs madly around Mrs. Upslovsky, pulling Dee in closer and closer to the lady who is wildly hitting the air with her umbrella. Dee ducks; finally, she just lets go of the leash and Bo bounds, like a sheep, for the house. Dee grabs his leash and yanks him in.

"He . . . he . . ."

"Warfield!"

Warfield, still on the phone, grins; catches on-- "What? The dog took a leak on your leg?" He starts to laugh. "Ah, Bobo's just marking his territory."

"Warfield, it's not funny. "

"Your dog . . . he sprayed . . ."

"Look, he's not my dog. He's Dee's dog."

Mrs. Upsky, I am so sorry." She offers her a tissue out of her purse. "Here."

Mrs. Upsky pecks the dog on the head, "Bad dog. Bad dog. Humph." Then, she accidentally opens the umbrella which shoots up, pops lose from the metal springs and belly flops inside out, leaving an exasperated Mrs. Upsky holding an umbrella like a melted popsicle.

Warfield pushes Dee towards the cab, politely smiling at Upsky and talking on the phone, "Warfield Swan, oh, great to hear from you. Can you, listen, can you hold for a second? My wife and I are taking off for a little house-hunting trip. The taxi's here. No, don't hang up." He covers the receiver. "Dee, get in the taxi. Ah, I forgot my laptop." He starts up the sidewalk towards the house.

Dee holds her ground. "Warfield. Just a minute." She turns to Josh. "We'll only be gone three days, well, three days and four nights. Four nights and three days."

A large brown and white floppy-eared rabbit hops out of the house; sees Warfield and hops straight towards Dee.

"Get the rabbit, Dee." Warfield whips into the house.

Dee leans down and picks up the rabbit. "Chelsea, come here." The Russian woman suddenly finds her voice. "Hello. Hello."

"Oh, Mrs. Upsky. Hello. I am so sorry about Bo."

"My name is Upslovsky. Your dog . . . he just, he just, how do you say it, he took a leak on my leg."

"I am so sorry. He's never done that before. Bad Bo. Bad dog."

"He, he circled me. He, he sniff me. Then, he lift his leg and he, how you say it -- he, he . . ."

Chelsea eyes the Russian baby-sitter from across the street; Dee tries waving to her, holding the rabbit. "Chelsea, come get the rabbit."

"The dog sprayed you." Josh has a tight hold on Bo who is eyeing the rabbit. "Don't even think about it, Bo."

"Chelsea Rose? Come here. I want you to meet Mrs. Upsky."

"Upslovsky." She wipes her long, black skirt with the tissue.

"I can't. I have to change Baby Ghost's diaper." Chelsea isn't budging from beneath the canopy of the Banyan Tree.

Suddenly, Mrs. Upslovsky comes to life. "Baby! Oh I love babies. Babies I love!" She wrings out the tissue and hands the limp piece of wet Kleenex back to Dee who very politely takes it, smiling.

"Oh, did the Agency say we had babies? The boys are ten and eight and Chelsea's four."

"There's Baby Ghost." Josh scuffs the sandy ground with the toe of his untied tennis shoe. "He's uh, what, about one? Two max."

Dee shoots Josh a look. He looks up, "What?" She mouths him "Be quiet."

Warfield reappears, flying down the porch steps. It's unbelievable but he's not on either cell phone. The rabbit makes a mad hop that lands him on the inside of the screen door and his ears appear for a second through the rip in the screen then wiggle and make like magic--and the rabbit disappears. And so does Bo. Who, although he is deaf, has somehow managed to hear Chelsea tear open a package of Oreo Cookies over at the Banyan Tree Tea Party.

Warfield glares at Dee, "Dee, have you seen my lap-top?"

"Calm down. I'm sure you can get one on the plane. Now, Warfield, this is Mrs. Upsky from the Sitters' Service, "We Like Kids"--remember?"

"Upslovsky." She curls her tongue back around her front teeth which are not unlike those of the rabbit. Big. And ugly. Warfield, who could smooth talk his own kid out of an ice cream cone, turns on the charm. "Hello."

Clara is uncharmed. She wipes her coat with a tissue. "Upslovsky. Your dog, he, how do you say he . . . " She motions, lifting her leg. "Now." She hands Warfield the damp Kleenex. "Where are the babies?"

Dee sniffs through her bag and manages to come up with an entire box of Kleenex. "Warfield, Mrs. Upslovsky is from Russia."

Warfield shoots her a look. "Really? Couldn't tell from the accent. What part?"

"Kiev." Mrs. Upslovsky eyes Warfield with the same look she shot on the dog just before he circled and lifted his leg.

"Oh, like the chicken." Warfield chuckles.

"Chicken? No. No chicken."

"Chicken Kiev." Warfield presses the point.

"Chicken? No, no chicken." The chicken connection is lost on Upslovsky.

Dee, good-natured, natural and true to her sweet spirit, hands the dog to Josh and offers a slip of paper to Clara. "Well, here's where we'll be staying."

"No. Read. No. " Mrs. Upslovsky reaches up under her hat and presses loose pins into her flat, black (actually blue black) hair.

Dee hesitates, then hands the address to Josh, rolls her eyes. It's just about too much for the Taxi Driver who gets out, opens the back door and whistles. From out of seemingly thin air, the rabbit appears, hops in. Warfield side-steps around the Russian baby-sitter and makes for the cab. "Dee, Dee! Now. We're going to miss the flight."

"Just a minute, Warfield. Say good-bye to Josh."

"Sorry, Josh. I didn't see you." Warfield thumps Josh on the head, then growls ever so innocently at Mrs. Upslovsky and dives for the taxi

"How could he not see me?"

"He saw you."

"No. I'm like, I'm like this invisible kid."

"He saw you, Josh. Don't make such a big deal out of it " She kisses his cheek. "Bye."

He picks up her suitcase and drags it down the cracked, hot sidewalk. Dee starts to get it, turns--Warfield pulls her in.

"Go. Go. Drive." Warfield raps on the back of the seat. The taxi driver glances in his mirror; his eyes roll.

"Bye." Dee rolls down the window and waves, "It's only three days. Find the hamster."

As the taxi kicks dust. Clara Upslovsky trudges up the sidewalk. up the steps, hugging her huge black plastic bag. Chelsea, from across the deserted street, follows Baby Ghost up into the maze of the Banyan Tree.

Josh waves good-bye, watching the taxi melt into a line of colorful traffic. Then, suddenly, the taxi screeches to a stop. The back door flies open; out hops the rabbit. He lands on his tail, sits still as if dazed, then hops off. Josh whistles. The rabbit's ears twitch and turn slightly. He hops back towards the small house and actually beats Josh to the door.

Boy and rabbit hesitate, listening from the front porch to the silence. Josh leans down and looks through the open screen door. Inside, Mrs. Upslovsky is taking off her great, black overcoat There's a jingling sound--glass hitting against glass. And even in the muted light, Josh can see the bottles. One by one, Mrs. Upslovsky takes the bottles out of the coat lining and places them carefully down on the coffee table. She pops off a lid; a hissing followed by the click of a bottle top missing the trash can breaks the silence.

Chad slides down the narrow stair banister and lets out a loud whistle which sends Upslovsky into the television and scares her into a series of bubbling, loud volcanic hiccups.

"Hi." Chad looks at her. "Are you the baby-sitter?"

Clara hiccups. "Where are the babies?" She hiccups again.

"What babies?" Chad walks towards her. His huge, lank frame lunges towards the couch where he retrieves a bag of potato chips.

He points the remote at the television set and then, turns the clicker towards Mrs. Upslovsky. He presses hard; nothing happens. "Damn, the mute's broken."

"Give me that." Upslovsky makes a slight pass for the clicker which goes air-borne. "Hey, what's with all the bottles?"

"Medicine. For my ..." She hiccups. "Toothache. I have, how you say, heavy metal. Mercury in my teeth. Yes?" She opens her mouth, exposing her huge rabbit-like teeth and scares the holy carrots out of the rabbit who rips through the screen door and dashes up the stairs.

Mrs. Upslovsky burps. Pours herself a drink from one of the mysterious "mercury cleansing/detox" bottles and plops her huge bottom down on the one and only chair that has not been transformed, turned upside down or over up, into a fort. She leans forward, not an easy trick for a hiccupping over-weight, mercury-laden lady and picks up the T.V. clicker which suddenly turns on the television. "Ah, good. Is good. Now out. Outside. Outside. Go." She shews Chad away from the couch with her foot. Chad disappears back towards the stairs.

From the T.V., a sugary voice escapes, rising above children's fake giggles-- "Good morning Wonderful. Today, we're looking at how to make your child's birthday party sizzle with Sugar.

Mrs. Upslovsky opens a bag of white cheddar cheese popcorn, staring at Sugar, the T.V. hostess in a party hat shaped like an elephant. Between hiccups, Upslovsky pops in the popcorn, oblivious to Chad who is quietly loading a beebee gun. He takes aim. She ducks, quite by accident. She drops the clicker. The beebee whizzes past her blue hair, ricochets against the T.V. screen and bounces back, scaring the befuzzle out of Upslovsky who burps.

She turns; her eyes roll like pinballs set loose in a glass caged shooting arena. Thin, narrow black balls, her eyes pinpoint the culprit. Chad, sitting on the stairs, worn thin, thinly disguising spills of every possible potion (grape juice, chocolate milk, ice cream of all flavors)-- smiles. Downs his glass of milk and burps.

It might turn into nothing more than a burping contest between Boy and Baby-sitter. But Upslovsky rises, stumbles against the vacuum cleaner and turns the nozzle on Chad. A great whirring noise erupts from out of the bowels of the vacuum. This is a machine that has eaten grit, grime and once, a live bird named Lemon (sucked up by Dee while she was cleaning the cage. Blueberry, the other parakeet, went ballistic until Dee managed to blow Lemon out by attaching the nozzle to the reverse blower.)

Chad fires. Then escapes. Out through the front door. Past the rabbit and Josh.

Josh catches his arm, "Hey, Chad."

"Oh sorry, I didn't see you."

"What's in those blue bottles."

"Medicine."

"No way."

"Yeah, for her hiccups."

Upslovsky charges around the room with the whirring vacuum; as she rounds the corner of the couch, she sees (too late) the crouching hamster. He opens his little mouth. Wide. In a silent scream. As only a little wee hamster can ... but it is too late. Whish. The great whirring, parakeet eating machine sucks up Chocolate Chip. He goes down without so much as an eek. Exhausted, she weaves, sinks into the big, billowy sound. It is not unlike that of a dying squirrel. EEK-- in Russian, of course. Then, she wails, "Babies, where are the babies? Babies love me."

Then, exhausted, she sinks down into the chair. She sips her medicine, points the clicker at Sugar (on the T.V.) and pulls a small radio out of her huge bag. She turns it on, pushes her legs out (the chair can do tricks; get big, get long, go up, go down!). Christmas music floats into the pandemonium. And if she happened to notice, which she does not, the vacuum cleaner actually tilts, ever so slightly--as if breathing (as if something live were moving inside!)

Josh quietly opens the screen door. He empties the vacuum cleaner bag. A terrified Chocolate Chip dashes for his open cage. Over the radio, Pippa's voice melts sugar, "All right all you lovely bachelorettes Got a Personal from the North Pole. Santa's looking for love."

Josh pokes his finger through the hamster cage and gently strokes Chocolate Chip. The little hamster rolls over on his back, sticks his legs up and opens his mouth, showing his little teeth. He'd like to bite Upslovsky but what's a hamster to a T-Rex. "It's going to be okay, Chocolate Chip." Josh turns and stares at Upslovsky, now snoring.

"We got to get her out of here. Fast." The hamster flips over. Stares with his little black eyes straight up into Josh's eyes. "I don't know how. Maybe . . . yeah,. maybe she's the one. She could be living at the North Pole. No way, you think?"

The hamster blinks.

"No, really? She's too fat. She's too ugly. She's too . . . but she loves babies. She loves to eat. She's big. She's beautiful. She's out of here. Thanks, Chip."

The hamster wiggles his nose, then nose-dives into his bedding.

Josh grins, catches sight of his dad's laptop lying under the bag of hamster food. He picks it up and heads out the door.

Behind him, Upslovsky snores.

As he comes across the yard, Josh catches sight of bubbles floating down out of the Banyan Tree. He puts the laptop down and leans into the shadowed tunnel of twisting branches and fronds. A bubble hits him on the head; he smiles. Then, quietly, sits down and sends the e-mail--

"Santa, Clara is the one! She loves babies. And she loves to eat.

You two are perfect for each other. Peppermint Palm, Number Five. Look for the biggest Banyan Tree south of the North Pole." He hits the button. Then, gets on his bike and takes off, bombarded by bubbles.

Chelsea stands high up in the tree, waving her wand. "Fairies of the wind, with this wand, make Upsky disappear. Poof!"

She closes her eyes, scoots back towards the trunk and smiles, "Wow."

A cupcake with pink frosting and a chocolate heart waits at the end of the branch.

CHAPTER SIX

Fly-swatting, hiccupping Mrs. Upslovsky stares at the television screen, mesmerized by Sugar St. Claire, a gorgeous middle-aged woman wearing paper elephant ears, blowing out pink candles on a birthday cake. A cute little kid leans over and blows chocolate frosting and chocolate saliva all over Sugar's perfect made-up face.

He giggles.

Sugar does not.

Upslovsky pops another blue bottle open, points the clicker at the television set and then at the hamster who is busily burying himself in his pine-scented hamster straw. "Sh-sh-h-h!" The hamster pauses, freezes and dives into the straw. Upslovsky turns up the volume and Sugar oozes into the silence.

Then, without warning, Upslovksy--or rather the chair in which she is napping--tilts up, goes backwards and her legs shoot straight out. This little trick puts her out like a light. Only Chocolate Chip, the hamster, is awake. He tip-toes over to his drinking bottle, glances over at Upslovsky and stares, wide-eyed, at Sugar St. Clair.

The set for "Hints for Stay-at-Home Mommies" is colorfully adorned with children, ages three to five, blowing kazoos, wearing animal masks clambering for some of the chocolate cake. The cake is shaped like a zoo. The frosting of which Ms. St. Clair is now smearing into a Kleenex. Aware of the camera, she smiles, showing chocolate teeth.

"Bye-bye. Bye-bye." Sugar winks.

The T.V. cameras close in on a colorful banner that says "Happy Birthday."

From the back of the set, the voice of the T.V. director sarcastically parrots "And bye-bye to you."

Sugar freezes the fake smile for a count of three, then melts. She becomes transformed. Wiping the chocolate off her cheeks, she licks her fingers, staring at the children -- "Go. Shew."

Assistants scamper, collecting kids, escorting them off the set.

Sugar starts peeling off her elephant ears, her fake nose, earrings, high heels and begins pulling off the eyelashes. One eyelash lands on her nose. She rubs her sore feet, which are really, really big and stares into the now dark cavern of cameras and lights. "William."

Her voice echoes against emptiness. She sighs. Feels the eyelash and sticks it the elephant ears. "William!"

William, a delightful, elfin-looking young man with a goatee, slightly balding and a bit of glittery jewel stuck in his ear, appears.

He's quite thin, and somewhat anxious. Holding a note pad, a cup of coffee and chewing gum.

"There you are, William. How on earth do you chew gum and drink coffee at the same time?" She's on her feet, moving towards the nervous little man, popping gum. "I am never doing kids birthday parties again. I don't care how dreadful the ratings are."

She pushes her way through a sea of assistants, scurrying to dismount the Birthday Party set. There are tables for mask-making and cake decorating; foam hearts and sequins spill out of clay pots. It's all very colorful and pz-zazz!

Sugar steps around a young woman carrying a life-size paper mache lion piñata. "Who are all these people. Scat. Boo!"

William scurries to keep up with Sugar, "Lets' face it, bubbles, it's not like you can cook, sew or sing."

"Of course not, I'm the star. How's my hair?"

"Terrific. Your hair ... what color is that exactly?"

"Toasted almond. Do you think I should go red? She weaves in and around the cameras, heading towards a back exit. William follows.

"I don't think Sunflower Glory could save you, bubbles."

"My fans love me." She pulls off the eyelash stuck to her nose. "Except for my feet. Tell that horrible camera man not to point that thing at my feet." Sugar opens the door, flooding the studio with sunlight. Then, with a dramatic flip of her toasted almost hair, she pouts her rose-bud lips and smiles, "Fans don't care about big feet."

As she escapes out of the studio, she ties a scarf around her hair, and opens the door to a red convertible conveniently parked right outside.

William hugs the curb, coffee mug still in tow-- "Your fans are lucky to be on their feet. Bubbles, we're going to have to go for a different look."

She turns the key in the ignition. Revs the engine and starts applying red lipstick. Pippa's soft southern drawl plays on the radio. While Pippa's speaking of "lighting of your love-life", Sugar lines her lips with a finely pointed pencil. Speaking through thin lips, she hisses, "Do you think my lips are too, I don't know, much?"

William leans over and turns up Pippa, "Forget your lips, Bubbles. Listen."

And over the airwaves comes the rescue, "You heard it from Pippa. Santa's lonely. He's got a Christmas Wish List and you might be ..."

Sugar scowls, still looking in the mirror, and for the first time, sees the eyelash stuck on her nose. "Good heavens, why didn't you tell me?"

William turns up the radio.

"Mrs. Santa Claus? Oh please, William. Really, I'm too young!"

William shoots her a look.

"All right. I'm too thin."

"Just meet the guy."

"Is it anyone we know?"

"Who cares if we know him, Bubbles. It's probably some public relations trick by the radio trying to kick up ratings, but if we play it right, you'll be Mrs. Claus. A star."

"You think? Isn't she second-fiddle to the big guy?"

William opens the car door; Bubble's scarf is caught in the door. As he reaches down for the scarf, he gets a bird's eye view of Sugar's feet. He can't help but react; Sugar slams the door in his face--popping his bubble. She continues putting on her make-up. Christmas songs play on the radio. As the idea sinks in, Sugar actually youthens.

"My ticket out of South Florida--hm-m?"

"Straight to the top. 'Stay at Home Mommy' could become 'Creations by Mrs. Claus'. A make-up line; clothes!"

"Yes. Who would make them?"

"The elves, Bubbles." William winks.

"Oh, I see possibilities, here. Santa and I, partners? He has elves." She lowers her voice, "I have elves."

"You could go on tour. Give candy canes to orphans."

"What would I wear? He wears a'lot of red, doesn't he? I look terrific in red." She snaps shut her glittery gold compact.

"That's my Bubbles. Think big. Bold. Beautiful."

"And a Mrs. Santa Claus line of make-up. Lipsticks! Poinsettia pink, Candy Cane Coral and Simmering Snowflake."

"We'll get it in Wal-Mart!"

"Wal-Mart, my foot. Saks Fifth Avenue, Neiman Marcus, Nordstroms!"

"Whatever you say, Bubbles. Maybe come up with a doll!"

"Oh a little miniature me. With a crown and fur. All right, take care of it. Call Pepper." She revs the engine and motions William to get out of the way.

"It's Pippa. I thought we'd invite him to the Poinsettia Ball."

"Wonderful." She pecks the button, up rolls the window. Then, suddenly, down it rolls. "Oh but you don't think I'll have to kiss him. He has a beard. Well, no kisses until the beard goes. This time next year ..."

"Oprah. Rosie. Jay Leno!" William pops his cell phone out of his pocket; out drops a pack of Juicy Fruit gum. He dials, coming up from picking up the gum. "Oh hello. Hello. Yes, this is William Fairchild with 'Stay at Home Mommy Sugar St. Clair. Ms. St. Clair would like to invite Santa to the Poinsettia ball? That's St. Clair -- she's a former Miss America. Right? That's the one." He glances at Sugar's feet.

Sugar snarls.

William sighs. Turns off the cell-phone. "They're not taking responses by phone, Bubbles. They've had too many prank calls.

Looks like nobody's taking it seriously. Okay--we'll e-mail."

"Oh pooh on them. Here, I'll write my own bio. You take notes."

William unfolds his note-pad. She dictates.

"Dear Santa,

How are you sweetie! I'm Sugar as in 'Sugar St. Clair's Tips for Stay-at-Home Mommies.' I have a heart as big as the North Pole and exude confidence, with style. I could add a whole new look to your reindeer-elf line. Not to mention you, big guy. Please be my guest at the Christmas Poinsettia Ball." She takes a breath, glances up at William "How will he know me?"

William answers without thinking, "You'll be the one with the big feet." He goes into a coughing fit. "Seat. Sheet. You'll be wearing a red sheet."

Sugar hits him with her purse. "I'll be wearing glittering red. No man can resist a woman in red. Well, tootles. Call Pippa. Tell her we'll do lunch."

She blows him a kiss and pulls the red Jaguar out into the traffic, narrowly missing a City Bus pulling in straight ahead of her. She honks loudly at the bus and zooms off. Her scarf flies off her toasted almond "do", whips through the air and lands at the feet of a woman in a Winnie-the-Pooh red tee-shirt and matching fuzzy elastic waist ski pants.

This is Carolyn. And she has the same hair-color as Sugar.

Only her's is natural. And Sugar's is, well, like the stuff in the little pink and blue packages--"fake".

Carolyn Ramey is the real thing in every sense of the word.

CHAPTER SEVEN

"Come on, now. Lilly Mae, it can't be as bad as all that." Carolyn offers her one free hand to the young girl who is bawling.

"No Miss Carolyn, it's worse. I got the baby coming and no place to go. I came back here . . . we were living in California, outside of San Diego . . . and I moved in with mama. Well, mama took all the savings I had saved up. Stole it right out of my pocketbook while I was sleeping in the bed. How could she do that to me?!" The tears roll.

"Watch your step, Lilly Mae." Carolyn gives a slight push and Lilly Mae rolls forward. "Take that seat there, next to Gerald Dean.

"What? Where you sitting, Granny?" Gerald Dean blows the biggest grape bubble ever seen by Lilly Mae who stops crying just long enough to stare at the boy with a boom box glued up smack to his ear.

"Scoot, Gerald Dean."

Gerald Dean scoots just as the bus lunges forward sending Lilly Mae into a downward spiral that lands her smack next to Gerald Dean. Carolyn grabs hold of a pole, motioning to Gerald Dean. "And turn that thing off." Carolyn rolls her eyes, pointing to a sign that clearly reads "No Nothing or The Bus Driver Will Eat You."

"Some kid put that up there. That ain't for real, is it?" He turns down the music which suddenly melts into Pippa's voice-

"Hi all you snowbirds out there in Southwest Florida. This is

Pippa with 'Lovin', Lookin' or Leavin'.' You, or someone you know, could be living in Toyland with elves and reindeers. And all the hot cocoa your heart dreams of."

Carolyn kindly offers a tissue to Lilly Mae; then, she pulls a whole box of Kleenex out of her grocery bag. Lilly Mae sobs; she speaks in-between great wails and blowing her nose.

"So mama come all the way from California and she offered to stay until I could get back on my feet and then she got a phone call and next morning, some guy showed up in a pick-up truck and they lit out of there. And I don't know why she took Sadie Baby." Lilly Mae honks her cute little perky nose. ". . . that's my cat and all the money I had saved while working at Billy Bob's Barbecue."

Gerald Dean rolls his eyes. He pulls his baseball cap down over his nose, then pops in another Sour Grape Gumball and blows.

"Blow you nose, baby."

"Now my feet is all swelled up and I got nowhere to go and what with the baby coming . . ."

"Well you must come on home with me and Gerald Dean, child."

Gerald Dean's head snaps up; the bubble spreads across his nose and he rises like a kid who's been hiding out in the eye of a tornado-- "Whoa! Where she goin' sleep, granny? We already done got Marigold and Moo, and Pumpkin and C.J. and Jordan and Mildred and that damn Chihuahua."

Carolyn opens a can of pop and takes a sip, "She'll sleep in your bed, Gerald Dean. You can sleep with C.J."

"Ugh, C.J. wets the bed."

"Ms. Ramey, you're the sweetest lady I have ever know." Lilly Mae positively purrs through the damp tissue. Her eyes glisten.

Gerald Dean blasts the radio and Pippa sounds like she's moved into the city bus; all eyes of the various and sundry passengers riding Bus Number 42 now turn and beam straight at the Boom Box.

"Don't be shy. Santa's looking for a sweet young thing and we all know love is blind. So look at the lady sitting next to you right now--wherever you are. She could be Mrs. Santa Claus--with the right connections. Just give us a call. That's Pippa, Lovin', Lookin' or Leavin'."

The bus zig-zags to a sudden stop outside a row of cracker jack houses, painted various colors, hot pink to lime green and orange. But most of the porches are cracked and sagging and the wide asphalt streets bubble up as if alligators might be sleeping beneath the street. The air here is hot and heavy; as the bus door opens, a spray of No See'Ems push against the cool bought air on the bus.

Carolyn, balancing shopping bags bulging with everything from milk to hand-me-down shower curtains, gently guides Lilly Mae out of the bus. Lilly Mae swats at the no see 'ems circling around her face. Gerald Dean follows, eyes popping. They wait until the bus has moved off, kicking a fine grey-sand colored dust across their faces, and then make their way across the street. Scraggly trees stick up out of hard, sun-baked, or rather sun-fried earth. As they cross, one of the egg cartons breaks open out of Carolyn's sack and egg yolks ooze out over the sizzling hot asphalt.

"I'll have mine sunny-side up!" Carolyn laughs.

But Lilly May bursts into tears. Again.

Gerald Dean gathers up as many eggs as he can rescue and scoots ahead of Carolyn, heading towards a tired, red brick, house. The roots of a skinny banyan tree stick up through sun-parched grass. Mildred, an ancient woman with caramel skin, is planting plastic poinsettias in the hard earth. Seeing Carolyn, kids--of all ages and sizes, grandchildren, great grandchildren--pop up like dandelions, staring out of windows, peeping from around a cracked porch, dragging doll babies. One little fellow, playing with a dragon, opens the screen door and hollers, "What'd you bring us, granny?"

Carolyn takes Lilly Mae's arm, "Now sit down on the porch. And don't mind Mildred. She's loonier than a bird." She helps Lilly May over to the porch swing. The pregnant girl sits, flies back. "Now what you want for supper, baby? I got poke greens and cornbread, fried chicken, mashed potatoes and shoofly pie."

Lilly Mae eyes the screen door nervously where a fierce-looking Chihuahua is madly circling, barking, throwing himself again and again against the thin mesh. Gerald Dean makes a dash for the front door, whizzing past the dog and C.J. who shoves the dragon up in his face, "Move C.J. I got important business to do."

39

A young girl's voice squeals, "Where you fixin' to go, Gerald Dean? Don't you go to the bathroom. I'm fixin' to take a shower."

Gerald Dean, grinning, from ear to ear, shoots back, "I ain't goin' no where Chiquita, but Granny's going to the North Pole."

CHAPTER EIGHT

Candy-flavored bubbles float up out of Santa's Workshop at the North Pole. Suddenly, a bubble pops and a Teddy Bear parachutes down into a huge pile of mail carried by Cape. He balances the mail and catches the Teddy Bear, managing at the same time to open with his foot, the door into the Toy Workshop.

"Jingles! Mail." Cape glances around the workshop, filled with elves scurrying excitedly, chocolate bells ringing as they disappear down the little elves throats. "Jingles!" He tries to see over the top of the mail, making his way towards a desk with a computer.

Jingles, feet propped up, sits in front of the lap-top, licking a chocolate spoon, reading e-mail. There's an incredible pile of knee-deep mail around Jingles' desk. Cape steps around the mail and gingerly tosses the teddy bear, dripping with bubbles, onto Jingles' lap. The elf jumps, catches the bear and wiggles his ears. "Funny, Cape. Very funny. Put it over there. You're not going to believe the e-mail junkies out there."

"All this is from 'Lovin', Lookin' or Leavin'?" Cape lifts Jingle's legs and eases himself up onto the desk.

"Nope. Kids. We've only gotten three responses to the ad.

Everybody thinks it's a joke. Here." Jingles tosses Cape three letters.

Suddenly, Blitzen's antlers rise up out of the pile of mail.

"Cape, get the reindeer out of here."

Cape takes an apple out of his back pocket and bribes Blitz who bites it and doesn't budge. "Go on now, be a good reindeer."

The reindeer tosses his head; bells jangle. "Well, suit yourself. But no more apples." Cape lightly jumps down into the pile of letters and starts opening the first envelope, sealed with pretty hearts. Blitz reads over Cape's shoulder. He sighs, puts down the envelope. Glances at the addresses on several other letters.

"All from children. I can't believe this, Jingles. What's happened? Where's belief? Doesn't anyone older than eight think there's a real Santa who deserves a real darlin' for Christmas?"

"Let's concentrate on the positive, Cape. Full cup of Peppermint Cocoa. Go for the top three and don't tell anybody that the top three is the only three. Right? Right. Now where's Santa?"

Cape shrugs his shoulders, glances at Blitzen, "You have three?"

"We've got three. Where's the big guy?"

Blitzen turns his head, glancing up at a loft where Santa is merrily flying a newly designed toy llama. The llama, with lovely wings, soars out over the elves, circles round and nose-dives straight for Cape who ducks.

Santa takes off his glasses, wipes them and chuckles, "Cape. Send the llama back. Got to work on his wings. Name is Chillepop."

"Hello Chillepop." Cape gives the llama a toss.

Santa catches the stuffed animals and waves. Then he casually dips a delicious looking strawberry into some chocolate and smiles, with chocolate smudged mustache, beard and teeth.

"Good heavens, what's he doing?" Jingles glances at Santa.

"Eating."

"Again."

"It's his mid-morning snack. I like the llama, Santa. Great idea. A flying llama." Cape waves, smiling.

Jingles, however, is not a happy elf. He spins around. "Wait. Stop. Stop everything." He picks up a megaphone and shouts, "STOP!"

The elves freeze. Even Blitz freezes.

"What is it? You found her?" Cape whispers inside the megaphone.

"Look at him, Cape. He can't meet anyone. Not yet."

"Is something wrong?" Santa has stopped mid-air with dipping his strawberry.

"No, nothing wrong. Jingles just wanted to try out the new multi-lingual megaphone. See. Here goes. "Arrestez-vous. Yep, it works." Cape laughs. Santa laughs. The elves go back to work. Cape grabs Jingles' sleeve, with little silver bells jangling on the fringe.

"Why? Jingles. Whoa, elf. Why?"

"Because he's, well, he's the wrong shape."

"He's Santa Claus. He's supposed to be that shape. You know, 'a bowl full of jelly." Cape follows Jingles who is searching the Inter-net under Ya-hoo: Health, Nutrition and Exercise. "We're going to have to tone the belly."

"How? He'll get suspicious."

"I'm not talking changing the image--just recharging the battery." He clicks through diet options, Adkins, Protein Plan, Low Carb, hm-mm, Perricone Prescription (lots of salmon) . . . Santa's not really a fish lover. Slim Fast. Maybe." He spins around on his chair. "Lets' go for the charm. Get me the Dolls."

Cape flips through a Christmas Doll Catalogue, "Which ones? We've got the Baby dolls, the American Girl Dolls, the Madam Alexander Dolls."

"Nope. Babes. Get me the Barbies." Jingles picks up a cell phone. "Hello, Jingles. Right. We need some Barbies down on the Toy Floor. Let's see . . . send Olympics Barbie, Figure Ice Skating Barbie, Gymnast Barbie and Karate Barbie."

"Karate Barbie?" Cape shoots up an eyebrow. "I don't think we have one."

"Thanks." Jingles clicks off the phone. "I'll lead the class." He takes off, whistling. Starts stretching; limbering up. Cape puts an arm around Blitzen and they both shoot a look up at Santa who has now moved on from chocolate-dipped strawberries to a huge Candy Cane. He squeals with laughter, amused, delighted by the antics of a mechanical, wind-up dog. Santa holds out his hand, "Sit. Stay. Shake hands. Good dog." The little dog sits, shakes, and holds out his paw.

Santa laughs, happily licking his candy cane.

Cape meets the reindeer's steady gaze, "Blitzen, I don't think this is such a good idea."

Jingles turns on some Motown music; it's loud and practically blasts the elves out of their merriment. He rolls his neck to the right, then back to the left. "Cape, buddy, we're running out of time. Santa only goes down there once a year. He's got one shot and one shot only. We want that to be our best shot, right?"

Before Cape can answer, the Barbies appear. They are the life-size models for the dolls. Gorgeous. Peppermint white smiles. Gymnast Barbie is toting her parallel bar; Olympics Barbie chats with Ice Skating Barbie about her recent Gold Medal and Karate Barbie cracks a candy cane with an easy twist of her sweet fist.

In unison, in one big breathy smile, they greet Jingles, "Hello."

"Well, hello, Barbies." Jingles winks at Cape who blushes.

"Give me just a minute. Go ahead and warm up." He picks out some music, all the time jiving and breaking into a kick-boxing routine while singing out "Work it, Barbies. Work it. All right. I think I'm ready. Why don't you Barbies warm up while I go over a few details with Cape."

The Barbies begin to dance and work-out to the spirited music. Ice Skating Barbie spins round on her ice skates and skates figure eights around gymnast Barbie who is doing double back flips around Olympic Medalist Barbie who just keeps smiling at her Gold Medal. Karate Barbie stares with great concentration at the gold medal.

Jingles wraps his arm around Cape, "What we need is a scout."

"What?" Cape unwraps Jingles' arm.

"Someone to check 'em out first. We'll send the Big Guy in for the finish."

"You go. I'll lead the Barbies."

"You can't dance. You're all ears. Look, here are the top three." He pulls three letters out of his hat. "Go check 'em out."

"I'm an elf."

"So, like who isn't? If you go anywhere, just smile and cover your ears." Jingles waves to the Barbies, "Okay, Barbies, we got a little job here. Go get Santa." The Barbies take off for the loft.

"Now, Caperton. Here we go." He opens a letter penned on orange blossom scented stationery, "Sugar St. Clair."

Cape's ears wiggle, "Sugar who?"

"Does it matter? We're not looking for social connections. Says she's a former Miss America, hosts a popular kids' television show and likes toys. She's inviting him to the Christmas Poinsettia Ball.

Perfect." Jingles ushers a reluctant Cape towards the door. As they go out, he drops one of the letters. Blitzen, trailing behind, picks it up and follows the elves out into the Winter Wonderland.

Cape whirls, "Not so fast, Jingles."

"Take the sleigh. And you'll need a reindeer." He sees Blitz.

"Blitz! All right, you'll do. Oh and a tux for the ball." Jingles grabs a tux off a large stuffed teddy bear standing just outside the door to the Toy Workshop. Blitzen nuzzles Cape, trying to show him the letter that is dangling from his antlers.

"Not now, Blitzen. What do I say?"

Jingles pushes the sleigh out of a snow drift and harnesses Blitzen. "Relax, bubba. Just ask Sugar to dance. Call me. Here, take my cell phone. No long distance charges." He presses the phone into Cape's shaking hand.

"I don't think Santa will like this."

"We're doing this for Santa. Remember, he's lonely. Every year he gets a nasty cold. We're giving him a Mrs. Santa Claus for Christmas. We're the good guys, Cape."

Cape climbs into the sleigh, "I don't know."

Jingles tosses him a small emerald velvet bag. "Catch."

"What is this?"

"Sugar and Spice. It's good for three wishes." Jingles nods to Blitz and the sleigh lifts off. He runs beside the sleigh, waving, "Don't forget to call me. And three wishes. That's it, Cape. No more than that in the bag."

Jingles does a back flip then does a hot salsa routine in the falling snow. The Oldies Motown fades into the gentler sound of Blitzen's bells, jingling. Blitzen flies, tosses his antlers and flings the letter back to Cape who catches it. Cape settles back into the seat of the sleigh, opens the envelope. A tad suspicious, he sniffs the letter, written on a torn piece of notebook paper, then reads aloud,

"Yo Santa,

I hear you're looking for a woman who can cook.

Stop by and taste my granny's chicken and dumplings.

p.s. If you choose granny, do I get more toys cuz last year I didn't get nothing except an orange.

I'll trade Mildred's Chihuahua for a reindeer.

Yours truly,
Gerald Dean."

Cape sighs and turns over the envelope, "There's no address."

The reindeer snorts; Cape turns the letter over. "Oh, here it is. 561 Cane Run Road. Well, we've got Sugar, Granny and who's this?"

He glances at the third envelope, neatly addressed. "No name. Just an address. Number 5 Peppermint Palm."

The sleigh circles stars, dips down over the tops of trees.

Between the tall graceful palms, Cape catches a fleeting glimpse of an abandoned Amusement Park. The sleigh casts its shadow against an old Ferris Wheel, sighing like a lost child, as it catches the wisp of wind. Then, a merry-go-round takes shape in the thick blanket of overgrown fern and windblown grasses. And visible only for a moment, a boy, riding his bicycle, disappearing deep into the darkness of the deserted park.

CHAPTER NINE

Josh pedals his mountain bike faster and faster. With great abandonment, letting the wind whip through his thin shirt, he stands and lets go of the handlebars. Fearless. Heart beating wildly. Alone in the thick shadowy coolness of a secret place. Above him, a metal sign leans sideways as if it too had shouldered too heavy a burden and finally slipped beneath the weight of wind and time. It reads in painted black letters "Jungle Larry and Safari Jane's.

Josh slips down, onto the seat of the bike; he grips the metal handlebars, sticky with sweat, warm beneath his fingers. Breathing with the bike, becoming one with the exhilarating motion, he cuts up a broken asphalt path, overgrown with milkweed, ferns and the wild orange flowers that drench the mist with their sweetness He circles in and around a playground. Rusting and wrapped around the strong poles, the swings have long ago lost their seats. The high slide is now slightly bent and a funny looking alligator sea-saw is absent its tail. Josh rides on.

He knows this park. He knows the curious labyrinth of twisted concrete road and disappearing foot-trails. This is his portal into a secret place where there is no past, no future -- only this moment.

He heads towards a distant Ferris Wheel; suddenly, but not unexpectedly, the bike goes airborne up and over old train tracks. The playground melts into shadows; the giant metal gods of the old amusement park rise up. Solemn. Ageless, time-worn priests of a playground abandoned to wind and boys running away to a hidden place where the heart is safe.

He rides slower now, staring up at the Ferris Wheel. It is unbelievably high. He leans his bike down into the soft sandy earth and slowly walks towards the lowest swing, just above his reach. He begins climbing, up the center, moving in and out of the lattice poles. Once, he loses his balance, catches hold with one hand and swings out from the metal rim. The wind sighs, sounding plaintive, deceptively safe--purring as some lost kitten left out in the cold. He hesitates, dangling out--riding the wind. And there is a moment, brief, yet eternal, when he almost lets go ... when he goes deep into the pain of his aloneness and faces the black abyss.

And it is at this very moment that a curious coincidence takes place in that abandoned amusement park. A woman, attacked by a wild and ferocious, if unseen, animal cries out--

"Help! Help!"

The human cry slips through the silence rising up in waves around Josh's heart. It slips through the portal of his aloneness and tears him back, back towards the Ferris Wheel. Back towards the cool metal and the tingling sensation of fear that suddenly shoots up through his legs and arms as he pulls himself up onto the narrow ledge and stares straight down into the thick undergrowth.

"Help! Help!"

Josh turns his head, trying to see down. The light plays tricks, glints off the metal seat of the Ferris Wheel, now swinging back and forth, as if caught in the irons of the wind. Josh shields his eyes and stares down. There, in feathered light that is almost amber in the coming dusk, a woman stands, shielding her eyes, staring up at Josh. She seems almost to be watching the boy as the boy watches her. Then, as if sure of her intended audience, she moves in rapid circles, swinging out her purse, hitting at whatever or whoever might be circling around her.

Josh climbs back down the Ferris Wheel, weaving in and around the swings which are now all turning, beating the air in sync with the woman's wild swinging of her purse. He jumps, lands in the tall weeds and offers his hand to the woman, who is now lying or rather half-sitting in a deep pile of brush.

"Ma'am, are you all right?"

The woman's eyes speak of a thousand secrets; filled wih a light and innocence that suggests she is herself a child playing dress-up in the costume of an old lady. Piacing one finger to her lips, she whispers, "Sh-sh-h."

Josh kneels down, glancing around nervously. "What happened?"

Eyes bluer than any eyes Josh has ever seen in a grown-up's face crinkle against the light and in a hoarse, breathy voice, the woman whispers, "Snipe."

"What? Where?" Josh's slightly southern drawl slips out as he stares in disbelief at the woman. But she shakes her head, eyeing the branch of a tree slightly bent, sighing, as if it too had been a witness to the attack.

"It came straight out of the fern. Scared the wozzle out of Whisper."

"Whisper?"

Suddenly, a skinny, really skinny black and white greyhound, panting hard, emerges from out of a sandbox. The dog licks Josh's face, his hands and wags his tail.

"If you would be so kind?" She holds out her hand and Josh pulls her up and out of the dense wildflowers and ferns. She straightens herself, places her hands together in front of her heart and bows her head, in a blessing. She seems even smaller, standing and laughs, with a wonderful, child-like laugh that makes the dog howl.

"Goodness honey, that was quite a fright. Wasn't it lucky you were here. I'm Nana. This is Whisper."

Whisper sits, holds out his paw. Josh shakes the dog's paw, "Josh."

"It's a pleasure to meet you, Josh. Now where on earth are the lemons?" She brushes off her flower-print dress, and limps over towards a large basket over turned in the high grass, spilling lemons. Suddenly, her ankle gives way; she catches her breath and stands still. Josh, still a little uncertain about the curious stranger and her dog, follows at a short distance.

"Maybe you should just sit down . . ."

"Oh goodness, there's no time for sitting down." She leans over and begins picking up the lemons lying scattered in and around the thick orange flowers. "We've only three more days. Here, put them in my apron. The basket's done broke."

Josh helps pick up the lemons, turning each one in his palm.

"You sure these are lemons? I've never seen lemons this..."

"Small?"

"Yeah, scrawny. And green."

Nana smiles, tossing one gingerly to Whisper who catches it, then rolls it between his paws, and finally tosses it back into her apron. "The worth of a lemon is not in its color or its size, is it, Josh?

"I don't know. I don't really eat 'em. Did you come in here just to pick lemons?"

"I'll tell you a secret. I come here every year for these lemons. For the Shaker Lemon Pies. This is the only place I know of where you can find lemons this sweet. And no one minds--why, who else eats lemons? Not the flamingoes . . ." With this, she gestures to a flock of pink birds, perched on skinny pink legs, staring silently. "Certainly not the snipe." Nana throws back her head and laughs, "Got to add the sugar, cream and eggs before a snipe will even sniff a lemon." She glances at Josh, still suspicious about the lemons. "Would you like to see the tree?"

"The tree?"

Without answering, Nana pushes back some ferns and makes a path through the dense undergrowth. Josh, skeptical, follows. Nana steps back. Josh glimpses sees a solitary tree, in the shadow of towering pine trees. Radiant. And vibrating, actually moving, shooting out auras of golden light.

"What do you see?"

"A tree. A lemon tree?"

"Are you sure?"

"Yeah. I guess they're lemons."

"I'll show you a secret. Crinkle your eyes. Close them, slightly. Gently. Now open slowly. See with Whisper eyes." The dog purrs.

"Whisper eyes. It's in the ancient, sacred books. Seeing life this way, ah--coincidences happen. Miracles happen. Life comes to us without us really having to try. But the trick, what's not easy, is letting go of the handlebars, trusting, riding with the wind. Now, what do you see, Josh."

"I still have my eyes closed."

"Open them."

Josh steps closer in towards the gnarled old tree, blazing with a curious white light that stretches out from the tips of the branches, burning out from the lemons.

"Wow." He holds his hand up towards this light.

"The lemon tree has an essence, a spirit. The Shakers saw this. In their drawings, their poetry, they spoke of a Burning Tree of Life."

"But how did ..."

"I'm not sure how or why this particular lemon tree came to be here in this old park. But they used to make movies here, back in the fifties. Maybe one of those films needed a lemon tree--with a twist." She laughs. And her laugh seems to blow softly across the branches of the tree; the lemons shine, almost translucent. Josh stands still, staring, fascinated by the tree which has been transformed. It stands no longer arched and bent but rooted deeply in the earth, its branches embrace the wind and light as a dancer arched and rising slowly into a light that is so fantastic, so other worldly, it seems almost to transform the coming dusk into dawn.

"Something kind of sacred about this old lemon tree. Like you're standing in the presence of angels." She gazes at the tree, up through its branches. "Gracious, looks like ... snow?" She touches one of the higher limbs, pulls it down and blows gently on the lemon. "Why it's sprinkled with snow. I wonder ..."

Nana and Josh glance up towards the sky. Dusk is closing in, and there's a mist rising from off the ground. They listen and the sound of the wind bending back the branches of the trees has just the slightest tinkling, as if the wind knew a secret.

Nana Hawkins places the last lemon into her basket with a sigh, "Curious goings on ... yes, very curious."

Then Nana moves on, back through the ferns towards the distant path. "So, why do you come here, Josh?"

"What? Oh, I like to be alone sometimes. That's all."

"Well, it's a good thing you do because if you hadn't come here today, I might have ended up snack for a snipe."

Josh picks up a small lemon, lying in the grass. He turns it over his hands, then offers it to her, "I think that's the last one. I better be ..." He glances around. "Do you have a car? Or a bike?"

Nana shakes her head.

"How'd you get here?"

"One good leg, one not so good leg. And Whisper. She's color blind and a little deaf but she has the heart of a great greyhound."

Josh watches Nana pick up the basket of lemons, she smiles, gives a curious little salute and starts back up through the waist-high grass. Suddenly, her ankle gives way and she loses her balance. The basket tilts; she steadies it against her hip and lets out a low gasp of pain.

Josh goes to her, taking the basket and offering her his arm for support. "You should probably get someone to look at that ankle."

She suddenly sits right smack down in the grass and sticks out the hurt ankle. "Would you be so kind?"

"Not me. I'm just a kid. I don't know anything."

"Why you're a Child. You know everything. The wisdom of a child, Josh, comes from the soul."

"Well, just to be safe, why don't you let someone take a look--a grown-up. " He steps back.

Whisper nudges Josh, licking his hand. Nana lowers the hurt foot, sits back, studying Josh as if wondering whether to trust him with a secret. "I don't believe in being safe. Josh, I'll let you in on another secret. I live by myself at the back of a Banyan Tree with a band of skinny orphans. And if I go to the hospital, there will be good people who will ask a'lot of questions and then, I'll be "safe" but who will take care of Rudolph and Prancer and Blitzen?"

"You live with a bunch of skinny reindeer?"

"Heavens no, honey. Greyhounds!"

A whippoorwill calls out; and somewhere close a woodpecker's voice taps against the gathering mist of stillness. Josh glances up, towards the woodpecker as if it reminded him of something, of a time outside the amusement park. He glances around, looking for his bike. Nana slowly rises, leaning on the good foot. Josh gets his bike and follows her.

"You're never going to make it with that ankle, Miss Hawkins.

How far do you live from here?"

Nana's back straightens; she turns her blue eyes, blazing with a curious light, on the boy, "Do you know the old Banyan Tree near the Pier?"

"The one with the black snake?"

"The very one."

"Yeah. I know it. I live there."

"Well, what a coincidence. So do I!"

Josh ducks beneath the low-lying frond of a crooked palm tree; he catches up with Nana, "No way? Behind the Banyan Tree?"

Nana doesn't stop walking. Her footsteps touch the sandy earth lightly, leaving almost no impression, except for an occasional missing flower which she gathers, adding to the lemon basket. "Number Five Peppermint Palm! Or is it Four? I can never get that straight. Something about mixed up numbers being painted on the wrong . . . oh, who cares about numbers? Do you think you could help me as far as the Banyan Tree, Josh?"

Josh hesitates, glancing at Nana, then at his bike. Again, the whippoorwill speaks to the woodpecker and then a whole trill of songbirds scatter their song, caressing the dusk. "Sure."

Nana climbs aboard and Josh has the feeling that he has known Miss Hawkins much longer than the short time in the park. They walk, she on the bike, in silence, back along the path but in truth, there is no path--just the trail of their footsteps and the soft impression of the bike wheels smoothing leaves, sand and wildflowers. And if a stranger or a clever snipe should happen to spy upon the curious pair, he or she might well think, "Ah, they are playmates." For there is a connectedness between them that takes no mind of age.

"Wind Dancer." Nana's voice breaks the stillness.

"What?" Josh stares over his hunched, frail shoulder.

"She's a good bike, eh?"

"Yeah, but how did you know her name?"

"Isn't it painted . . . yes, on the back?"

"No." Josh picks up speed, guiding the bike and its ride around the limb of a river birch that lay sprawled across the dip of soft earth. "The painting all peeled off. The name's invisible. . . . unless you knew what it was and then, maybe . . ."

"Really?"

"Yeah."

"What a coincidence."

Josh pulls his windbreaker tighter about his neck and he might have pursued her curious knowledge of the bike's name further if suddenly Whisper hadn't gone absolutely berserk. Wild yipping, bouncing of paws against the air that, as they neared the edges of the cool canopy of towering pine now grew thick with no see 'ems and sticky with the salty spray of sea air. Nana places one hand out calmly, "Down. Whisper. It's all right. Leave the snipe alone."

Josh glances at the greyhound, transformed into a bouncing yoyo, "What snipe?"

"Keep moving. Whisper's a former racing champ. Won the Texas Derby. I had the Superfecta and we bought real vanilla for the lemon pies. But she's very territorial and of course, hates anything that reminds her of that silly mechanical rabbit from the track. Lucky!"

Whisper dashes madly in and around the bike, pawing the sand, covering the bike's tracks. Then she takes off into a deep ravine, howling. Josh turns the bike straight towards the entrance gate to the park. Just as he reaches for the rusted iron lock, he sees something. A small animal, brown with eyes staring straight at him. In his paws, the little creature carries a lemon. The animal's yellow almost amber eyes stare solemnly. As if daring Josh not to believe, or perhaps, daring him to believe. It is a deep knowing stare. As if the snipe demands that the boy see what he thinks could not possibly exist. Josh, for the first time in his life, feels that he is actually being seen. Neither the mythical creature nor the child feel invisible. And in that brief, fleeting moment, time becomes fluid. The trees expand, reaching into the vast expanse of sky. The flowers and vines become more vivid, brilliant in color, rich in texture. And the Stillness, like a mirror catching the light of distant mirrors, dances.

Only Nana's touch, a human touch, spins Josh back into present time.

"The bike wheel's stuck. Should I get off?"

"Oh no ma'am." Josh gives the bike a good shove and Wind Dancer rolls forward, out the gate with Nana holding on-

"Oh. Oh."

"Is that what it's like?" He runs, catching up with the bike, grabbing hold of the bars. "Seeing, ya know, with . . . ?"

"Whisper eyes?"

"Yeah."

Nana nods. "Something like that. Shall we?" She sticks her legs straight out from the bike, then scrapes the soft sand with her open-toed flip-flop. "Whoa, I need my sunbonnet and sunglasses. I freckle."

Josh glances at her youthful face, rubs his nose, "I got some myself."

"Sprinkling of star-dust, gives the face character." Nana leans forward and honks the bike's horn. Josh, suddenly self-conscious, faces Nana. "Which way to the backside of the Banyan Tree?"

"Oh, I prefer the alleys, honey. Never can tell what you might see in a back alley. Airing dirty laundry lets sunlight fill the soul."

"What about Whisper?"

Suddenly, Nana lets out a low, playful whistle with a trilling burp, "Whisper. Here comes Lucky."

There's a rustling noise, a bending back of ferns and wildflowers and then-- Whisper, panting. Holding a lemon in his mouth. "Good dog." Nana takes the lemon and places it in the bike basket, then she ties her bonnet, wraps a scarf around her neck, pulls down the sunglasses, sticks out her legs, wiggles her toes (painted polka-dot red and green) and laughs, "Lets' boogie."

Josh guides the bike along the main road, Highway 41, then cuts into a tight alley lined with colorful gingerbread cottages. A lavender gate, overgrown with hot pink bougainvillea opens into a secret, hedge-lined garden. Further on, the bike splashes through mud from an errant lawn sprinkler and a Bed & Breakfast, in cream yellow with lime green trim, offers nose-tingling smells of baking chocolate chip cookies. Nana knows all of these cottages and calls them by name -- christening each with the name of a famous Greyhound. The alley winds in and around date and coconut palms and thick ferns, leading past high fences and an occasional gate that offers a glimpse into well-manicured lawns and sometimes a bathing pool.

"Look!"

Josh slows the bike, uncertain what it is that he's being directed to "look at". Then he sees it. A star, burning on the horizon, growing brighter and brighter until, against the canopy of coming dusk, Josh glimpses what looks like a sleigh, drawn by a reindeer.

"Is that what I think it is?"

Nana slips her sunglasses down off her nose, "Must be making some kind of trial run."

"That's impossible."

"Is it?" Nana turns her eyes, speaking secrets, towards Josh, "How long has it been since you believed, honey?"

Josh scuffs the sand with his untied tennis shoe, "Believed in what?"

CHAPTER TEN

It is almost dusk. A pale vapory mist rises up from the fronds of two tall palms as Cape guides the sleigh down, narrowly missing a cocky seagull. Honking, protesting noisily, the gull gazes aghast at the sugary sprinkling of snow on his wings and tail feathers.

"Christmas, Blitz! Ya almost got the beak of that bird."

Undaunted, Blitzen glides gracefully down for the landing.

Cape pulls the sleigh up in front of a wonderful ancient and incredibly secretive Banyan Tree. Cape glances up through the papery fronds of the tree, "She's a beauty this Banyan." He whistles, takes off across the hot black asphalt, heading towards the Cottage. Just as he steps off the curb, he catches sight of the numbers painted on the edge, whistles and glances back at the tree.

Blitzen watches the elf with half-closed eyes. He rolls the pistachio back and forth on his tongue. The reindeer clearly knows something Cape does not. Cape catches on. "All right. All right, Blitz.

What is it?"

Blitzen pokes at the letter in Cape's back pocket. Cape takes out the letter, re-reads aloud "Number 5 Peppermint Palm. Well, if this is Peppermint Palm and that's Number 4 and a half over there, across the street. Hm-m-m. " He stares at the Cottage, then back at the Banyan Tree. "Yo, Blitz, am I missing something here? Is there like a Number 4 and a half hiding behind the tree?"

Blitz shakes his harness; there's a gentle tinkling sound, mixing with the rustling wind. "Where? No, really? Ya don't say?" Cap tip-toes closer to the tree. He sticks his head into the shadowy coolness of the tree's belly and pushes aside a fern, glimpsing for the first time the arbor, overgrown with purple wildflowers. He glances back, wiggles his ears and tosses Blitz a couple of cracked pistachios before disappearing into the tree. He scoots up onto a wide, smooth branch and swings down, landing on the back side of the Banyan Tree.

Cape shakes off a feathery frond that served as a parachute for his graceful ascent out of the Banyan tree. He tip-toes away from the tree, taking in the yard dotted with plastic pink flamingos. A couple of scrawny grapefruit trees cast their shadows across the grass-bare lawn that serves as the garden for a dilapidated beach cottage, peeling turquoise and pink paint. Cape comes down off his toes, staring at the shapeless thin grey shadows that appear from out of nowhere and everywhere. Nothing moves. No one breathes. Whispers without form, the shadows shiver, go down for a yoga "down dog" and stare at Cape who goes to his knees, mirrors the "down dog" pose and holds out his hand, "Hello fellows. Caperton Elf. I'm looking for Number 5 Peppermint Palm.

The largest greyhound, a sultry black dog with pinched ears, sniffs Cape. Licks his nose. Cape sneezes, then holds out a cracked pistachio. "I'm looking for a gentle lady. Responded to a radio personal, 'Lovin', Lookin' or Leavin'. Perhaps you fellows know her?"

The big black dog yawns.

"Yeah, you do?" Cape yawns and drops to the ground, stretches, somersaults and comes up eye to eye with the dog. He pats the greyhound who licks his ears and follows Cape past the other dogs up onto a screened-in porch. He knocks on the door. There's no response. Cape tip-toes over to an open window where there's a cardboard sign, "Welcome. Help Yourself. Remember, you may be the first but you probably aren't the last. Enjoy and leave a lick for the greyhounds."

Cape sniffs the soup. He dips in a paper cup and takes a sip.

"Delicious. Sweet Potato Soup. A little curry . . . " He takes another sip. ". . . some fresh coconut! He finishes off the soup and moves on to a pie. There's a piece already cut. Cape treats himself.

"Um-um-wow. Shoofly Pie. Melts right in your mouth. The Big Guy would love this. I love this." He helps himself to a second piece, then leans through the open window. "Hello. Hello! Anybody home. Great pie!"

Sensing an audience, Cape glances over his shoulder where the greyhounds, about eight or nine, sit on their skinny back haunches, watching. They stare first at Cape, then at the pie. Their ribs stick out through their almost transparent skin. "Gracious boys, you fellas look like you could sure use a piece of Shoofly Pie. The whole pie. Here!" Cape eagerly dips his fingers into the gooey pie and offers it palm-flat to the big black dog. One by one, the other greyhound come forward, licking Cape's fingers. "That's it. No more." Cape backs away, heading towards the Banyan Tree. He swings himself up onto a low branch, waves to the greyhounds who thump their tails, "Good-bye".

Then, he's gone. Disappearing back into the cool passageways of the mystical tree.

As Cape jumps down out of the tree, a bubble hits him smack in the eye. A small voice, belonging to the bubble blower, catches the elf unawares-- "Is that your reindeer?"

More bubbles float down out of the tree. Cape glances up. "Ah--yes." Through a cascade of shimmering bubbles, Cape sees the child. Blowing bubbles, upside down. "Hello princess."

Chelsea comes right side up. She holds the wand up close to her lips, ready to spray the elf with more bubbles. She hesitates, as if delighted by the recognition. She waves the wand up towards the sky and spills the bottle of bubbles, "Ought oh."

Cape catches a bubble on his nose, sneezes and changes the bubble into an exquisite butterfly that takes off.

"Oh." Chelsea leans down, upside down again, smiling into the elf's green eyes, "How do you do that?"

"What?" Cape pulls himself up to the branch, does a couple of chin-ups.

"And how did you know I'm a princess?"

"How could I not?"

"Oh, you're an Elf." She pulls herself right-side up.

"I am. And you're a Child."

They both stare at each other. Checking out ears, eyes and tilted noses. Then, at exactly the same moment, they hold out their hands and say, "Pleased to met you." And laugh. They laugh till all their funny-bones are tickled pink and then they wiggle their noses and their ears and do a little dance. (And remember, the reindeer is watching all of this and he's feeling slightly left out, so he very non-chalantly gives his harness bells a shake and Chelsea, hearing the music, suddenly stops. "Wow."

Panting, Cape digs deep into his pocket for something he can't seem to find, "Oh cappuccinos and chocolates, I've lost it."

"What?" Chelsea is delighted by the sheer presence of an Elf in her Banyan Tree. And she even begins to search her pockets, which of course she doesn't have since she's wearing quite a lovely princess gown. Never mind that she hasn't any idea what it is that she is looking for!

"No, here it is." Cape takes the crumpled letter out of his pocket. I'm looking for . . . "

Chelsea glances at the letter and even though she can't read, she recognizes the number, "Number 5 is across the street. They got the numbers mixed up. No one lives back there behind the tree. Who are you looking for?"

"The Lady of the Castle."

Chelsea giggles, "Oh, my mom's not home."

"Oh."

"She's with my dad. He's never home. They're looking for a house. Somewhere in . . . pretty far away. We're always moving. I've already lived in a bunch of different houses and I'm only four. Well, four and a half!"

Cape folds the letter. "Oh, well then she can't possibly be the one. I'm fairly certain the Lady in question is residing there now. Are you sure that's Number 5 Peppermint Palm?

Chelsea nods "yes." Cape looks terribly disappointed. She would like very much to cheer him up. "Maybe . . ."

"Yes?" He's all ears.

"Is there some other 'Lady in Waiting'?"

"Well, there is someone else."

Cape cheers up enormously.

"But she's taking a nap. Could you come back another time?"

Cape shakes his head, "Yes, but perhaps I'll just take a little peek." He starts across the street. Chelsea runs after him-

"Oh, Mr. Elf, I wouldn't do that."

Cape starts up the crooked stairs, steps onto the sagging porch and turns around--"Why not?"

"She smells." Chelsea holds her nose.

Cape hesitates. Quietly, he leans down and peeks through a hole in the torn screen window mesh. Inside, he sees a rather peculiar sight. A large, really large woman lies stretched out in a tilt-back chair. She is snoring. It is a sound unlike any sound the elf has ever heard. Except perhaps once--when flying over Iceland they came quite unexpectedly upon a gaggle of aging geese. The woman is wearing a curious coat--like a carpet bag with great drooping sleeves and she appears to be tied into the chair with twine. Although no twine is necessary, for the woman is quite out of it. Gooey honey sticks to her blue hair. A fly buzzes in and around her gaping mouth. Suddenly, she hiccups. Loudly. Her eyes pop open. She sits up. Stares straight at the window--and scares Cape who also hiccups.

Then, the woman falls back down into her honey-oozing, fly buzzing stupor. Cape turns around and sees Chelsea,

"Yes, I see what you mean. Well, perhaps, when she wakes up."

Chelsea jumps an imaginary jump-rope, "May I pet your reindeer, please?"

"Of course." Cape and Chelsea walk back across the street. Blitzen snorts a sort of "I told you not to bother with that one." and lowers his head for Chelsea to scratch his neck. Cape climbs into the sleigh and tosses Chelsea a handful of glitter that magically turns into a butterfly. Beating the air with ever so tiny, iridescent wings, she alights on Chelsea's nose. The little girl stares at the butterfly--delighted, "Wow."

And when she remembers to say good-bye, Chelsea sees the sleigh rising gracefully up, up into clouds shaped like candy canes. Cape waves good-bye. "I'll be back."

"How do you do that?"

Chelsea's words disappear into the sound of greyhound dogs barking loudly as the sleigh dips and soars above the Flamingo

Cottage. Cape tightens his hold on the reins, "Blitz, let's check out this Carolyn." He unfolds the scrap of paper. "561 Cane Run Road. Says she likes to cook. Grits and . . . " Suddenly, the reindeer nose-dives into a cloud-bank, circles round, kicking stardust.

"Blitz, slow down. Says here to 'bring the reindeer.'"

With a snort, Blitz gallops gracefully through the gathering clouds, leaving a trail of cracked pistachio shells.

CHAPTER ELEVEN

As they come out of the shadows of Jungle Larry's and Safari Jane's, Nana points towards the back alleys, leading across the highway. Josh guides the bike; and they begin the journey to Nana's home in silence. She nods, gazing always ahead, sensing rather than actually looking for the right path. Then, suddenly, the spacious lawns give way to narrow alleys. And as they approach a colorful cottage, lavender with yellow trim and a gate all splashed over with hot pink, Nana seems to suddenly youthen. She smiles at Josh, her blue eyes crinkling against the silver light.

And it is then that Josh senses a connectedness with this old, curious woman. She is indeed strange. Wizard, witch, winged being. More like a child riding her bicycle --more like an old lost friend whom Josh has always known and searched for and when he least expected, she appeared. The alleys are her secret haunts; she knows the names of the winding streets that lead deeper and deeper into a sea of green. Verdant and emerald and the green of fresh lime--swirl around them as Nana whispers the names of the trees overhead.

"The Tree of Gold"--Nana raises one hand over-head, sweeping the low-lying branch of a tree resplendent with yellow blossoms. "It is so beautiful, yes? The tree is dedicated to Saints." They ride on, past the Royal Poinciana with its burst of red flowers, breathing in the mystical secrets of the Jacanda Tree; its wispy foliage trails over their heads and they duck so as not to scatter the lovely bell-shaped petals. Up and over a bridge, they cross an inland water-way, and disappear into the cool shade of palms. Christmas Palms and the

Royal Palm, quite grand and tall ... date palms and pineapple palms--
all bearing a great resemblance to their names. Josh listens, amazed
by her knowledge of plants and trees.

As they draw closer to a park, right on the sea, Nana trills aloud
the names of wildflowers. A purple vine with paper leaves and lilac
colored flowers is bougainvillea. And the intoxicating scent of tiny
white blossoms that catch the light and taunt a thousand different
smells (each more delicious than the next) is honeysuckle. "Josh,
that's Bleeding Heart. The flowers are sometimes used in witchcraft
to attract something desired by the heart."

She winks and Josh watches as she snips off a small piece and
sticks it in with the lemons. "The story is that a young lady and her
lover quarreled and he left her. Sad and lonely, she wept. Years later,
he returned to find her. But she was gone and all that remained
were these tiny red flowers shaped like hearts, where her tears
touched the ground."

Lilies, of all colors and size, flame vine and bridal bouquet -a
shower of delicate white blossoms. "For your bride." She plucks
off a small bouquet and sticks it in her bonnet. "Never too old to
hope."

She sticks out her legs and holds onto her straw bonnet, flying
on the bike. Josh begins to see flowers and trees that he had never
before seen. The whole world changes--taking on a resilience that
he has somehow missed before. But Nana misses nothing. Then,
suddenly, the Gulf opens before them and she motions for Josh to
stop. He does. She lets her feet touch softly down on the sand and
for a moment they gaze out at the sea. It is very, very calm. And
the color mirrors the green of palms and honeysuckle hedge and
hibiscus leading down to the sea.

Then, Nana nods and they fly---back along the alleyway.

He guides the bicycle between a high leafy hedge and a wall. As
they continue through the alleyway, Josh becomes aware that Nana
is looking for something. Suddenly, she whistles to the greyhound.
Whisper turns, cocks his head. Josh looks around for some sort
of opening, a hidden passageway. The alley, narrow and secretive, is
bordered by a thick concrete wall on one side and on the other, a
fichus hedge. Nana, however, sees what is invisible to Josh.

A waxy plant glistens in the light. Nana stops, staring at the plant which looks quite ordinary to Josh. Then, she opens her straw basket and takes out a pair of spectacles. Leaning close to the plant, she suddenly exclaims, "Ah, yes." She cups her fingers around the leaves, showing Josh a slight cutting on the dark green. "This is a Pitch Apple, Josh. Sometimes it's called an Autograph Tree for if you plant it by the front door of a house, visitors may sign their names and the cuts on the leaves will remain visible for quite a long time--more than a year."

Josh looks at the markings on the leaves. "What's it say?"

"Oh, it says Jingle Bells. Now, somewhere in here there should be . . . " She pushes through the thick pitch apple leaves, searching for something and laughs, " Ah yes! There it is."

Josh maneuvers the bicycle in and around the undergrowth, and stares at a butterfly, perched in the middle of the fichus hedge. A Monarch made out of wood. Curiously, Nana places her hand around the butterfly and pushes. Surprisingly, the hedge swings forward, revealing a mysterious garden hidden behind the hedge. As Josh pushes the bike through the gate, he realizes that that particular part of hedge is not real; it's fake. Slips of green and tiny white flowers resembling the honeysuckle hedge are glued onto a piece of wood. The fake hedge becomes a tiny gate through which Nana and the greyhound disappear. But Josh, unfamiliar with the magical portal, leans down, hunching his shoulders, frog-jumping through the opening and scratching his bare arms. "Wow! How did you ever find this?"

Nana seems not to hear the question; she disappears into a yard filled with pink flamingos and an orchard of grapefruit trees.

It is a curious place; seemingly abandoned of any human life--a windswept garden scratched thin with prickly thorn-weeds and clouds of No See 'Ems hovering close to the hard ground. Wildflowers scatter color across the sandy earth, dispelling the sense of abandonment. It is a place tucked behind walls, hidden by towering shrubs-- a place undisturbed not so much because of luck but rather because it appears to the eye as a beach cottage worn thin by weather and wind, stripped bare of anything useful. And yet -- out of the silence, birdsong rises. A mourning dove whispers "Secrets."

Nana leans against Josh. Hopping on one foot, she guides Josh into a yard thick with grapefruit trees. They are quite old, and their branches are curiously twisted, their trunks bear the scars of having survived strong winds, perhaps hurricanes. They are all that remains of what must once have been a resplendent orchard. A sweetness mixes with the salty taste of sea air. Josh brushes his hand across his nose, trying to stifle the sneeze. He sneezes, rather loudly. Nana raises her hands up to her heart and in a somewhat odd gesture, bows her head. "Mun-gu-aku-bariki."

Just inside the gate, Josh sees an old, really old and weather-beaten mailbox, shaped like a flamingo. A metal palm tree waves fronds over the pink mailbox. About a dozen plastic pink flamingos stick up out of the hard earth. As they wander up through the yard, a mixture of sand and trailing wildflowers, Josh suddenly sees the greyhounds.

They are silent. They shiver, excitedly. Staring. Nana releases Josh' shoulder, "It's all right. He's with me." She gives a slight gesture of her hand and suddenly the dogs abandon any pretense of manners and greet Nana and Josh with wild abandon. Shaking. Thumping tails. Licking Josh on his face, his hands, his ears. Nana throws out her arms, "Hello, Sugar-Belle, missed me? Now, here honey, get down. This is our new friend, Josh."

One of the skinniest greyhounds, a light tan dog, goes down on his front paws and grins at Josh.

"He's asking you to play." Nana rummages through her pocket for bits of cracker which she tosses out to the dogs. Grateful, they sit down on their haunches, wait and only when given the signal by Nana do they eat the treat. Josh scratches the tan dog between his ears, then on his chest. The dog rolls over, thumping his tail. Josh leans down to the dog, tickles his belly and for the first time, he catches sight of the Banyan Tree, sprawling up like a fantastic giant parasol, feathering golden light out onto the flamingo yard.

"Cool. This is the backside of the Banyan Tree."

"Did you know, Josh that it was under a Banyan or Bode tree that the Buddha first received enlightenment. Such trees are very mystical. In India, the people believe that the spirits of those they once loved reside in the branches of the Banyan; so, you see, they never cut off a bough for fear of cutting off an ancestor. The roots shoot out and walk on their journey--for a hundred, two hundred years, across several acres of land."

She places her hand against the smooth bark of the old tree, then places both of her hands over her heart and bows in a blessing to the Banyan. Josh steps back, gazing up into the tree--catching hold of a dangling root. "Cool. I didn't think there was anything back here, except for the black snake."

"Oh, there's a black snake all right. And he's big and if you don't like snakes, he might be kind of scary. But Stella's a cow snake. She keeps out the rats and helps keep the greyhounds safe. She's what I call one of 'God's angels in disguise.'"

Josh catches a glimpse of a sign, placed between two boards, blocking the path onto the property. It says in glaring yellow and black, "This Property Condemned." He steps back, catching on for the first time that the Cottage belongs to another piece of property. Faintly visible through wisps of hanging moss and dangling wildflowers is Palm Cottage, an historic landmark in Naples.

"Is this part of Palm Cottage?"

Nana nods, "Yes and no. Palm Cottage is lucky. It's on the National Register of Historic Places, but no one remembered the little Shell Cottage. So--" She gestured to the sign, sighing. "Well, lets' get those lemons up in the shade." She turns and limps towards the Cottage. It is two-storied with screen-porches on both levels. Painted flowers in pots and vines and birds decorate the Cottage's walls. A greyhound peeks out from behind bougainvillea. And along the trim, seashells give a finishing touch. Sand dollars and conch shells mix with turkey wings and starfish. Josh lets out a low whistle- "Wow. This is fantastic! Who did this?"

Nana pushes back her straw bonnet, "I did."

Josh looks at her. Awed. "Wow." He reaches up, touches a sand dollar, grinning. Slowly, he moves from flower to flower, amazed by her gift.

"It's not finished, of course." She gestures to a small piece of white-washed wall and a can of paintbrushes. "Perhaps, you'll do the honor of finishing the canvas."

Josh picks up a paintbrush, slips it through his fingers, and then looks up-- "But, if this is condemned, it will be torn down, right?"

"I suppose."

"But then why ... why do you do this? The painting, the seashells?" He tries to control the rising anger in his voice; and even Josh doesn't understand why he's angry. He kicks his untied Nike tennis shoe against a vine climbing up one of the slender palm shoots.

"Careful, that's a Night Blooming Cereus. A cactus. It's a vine and has splendid petals but the flowers only begin to open after it is dark. With darkness come their full bloom. Then, at the very first hint of morning light, the petals start to wilt and fold and soon disappear. Each Night Blooming Cactus has only one night of the year when its blooms open to the stars and moonlight. The cactus owns that moment; for a brief, stunning breath of time, she is Queen of the Night. In China, I'm told, they hold parties just to glimpse the magnificent blooms."

Josh casts his eyes away from the cactus; dragging his tennis shoe in the sand, marking an impression in and around the climbing vine. He waits. Knowing that somehow the strange cactus is Nana's answer to his question. Knowing also that there is more to the answer--he digs his hands deep into his pockets. Listening to the stillness that wrapped around him, around the whisper of blooms just appearing on the curious Cactus, around Nana. The strong leaves of the Banyan lift, facing the wind.

Nana also faces the wind. Coming from the Gulf. Josh knows at some deep level that his question has touched on something very deep and close to her whole philosophy of life. She closes her eyes, then opens them. "Because Josh, this moment is all I have. And in this moment, I try to paint joy. Paint beauty. Without thinking about what may have once been or what may be ... now. This is my gift to the moment." Then, she looks at him, with that same deep knowing, "It is all any of us really has. Just this moment."

The paintbrush slips through Josh's fingers and lands with a soft thud on the sand. As he leans down to pick it up, Josh notices a tiny flower. Blooming in the hard earth. He had almost crushed it with his foot. Now, seeing it, he wonders what else he might have missed in his life of eleven years.

"Lantana. The color of the flower changes; at first it is yellow and then it turns to orange and then from orange to red. Here." Nana reaches down and picks it, offering it to Josh, palm-flat.

Josh takes the flower and smiles, just slightly. He meets her eyes; they mirror light. An intense brightness that speaks of great kindness. "I've got a lizard back home can do 'bout the same thing."

"Oh really?"

"Yeah. He's from Argentina. My dad picked him up from a guy at the airport. Couldn't get the thing through Customs." Josh laughs.

"What's his name--this colorful creature?"

"Mr. Lantana."

"I should like to meet Mr. Lantana someday. Now, come on, we better get those lemons up onto a table or else we'll have hot lemonade."

Nana walks, limping over to an old, weather-beaten table, brushes off yellow moss and mold, whistling. Trailed by the smallest of the greyhounds, Oliver, Josh unloads the lemons, setting the basket down onto a table in the scant shade of a scraggly grapefruit tree. Josh steps in and around the flamingos, "What's with all the flamingos?"

Nana laughs, glancing at the metal birds. She doesn't answer straight off, instead, she fills a metal pie pan with water from a plastic container. Then, she splashes some water on the trailing flowers; the tiny petals open. Purple, lavender and hot orange burst out, rippling across the parched earth. Nana waves her palms across the blooms, in a curious gesture--as if drawing some of their energy and color up into the essence of her being. Then, slowly, she fixes her eyes on Josh, "The flamingos . . ." she pauses. Takes off her sandals and washes off her toes. Josh hesitates, then slips out of his hot tennis shoes.

" . . . well, a couple of free spirits lived here before Emma blew through. And, I reckon those fellas had a liking for pink, skinny legged birds. I can't think why they might have put a flock of them here, but I can't think of any reason to take 'em out. Can you?"

Josh shakes his head.

"Well, come in."

She opens the screen door and slips inside the small cottage. Josh follows, stepping into an unexpected steam bath. There is no electricity, not even a fan to move the heavy air. But Nana seems to take no notice of the heat. Heat without breath. Heat without a pulsing rhythm of life. Josh stares at the Cottage walls, the floor. A few white candles lie scattered across a yellow pine table bulging with newspapers, mostly pages with cross-word puzzles most of which have been worked and re-worked. Only a few white spaces spot the pages. The yellowing newspapers lie stacked up in corners of the room, serving as easels or display tables for paintings. The paintings are abstracts, vivid faces with eyes staring--some with third eyes and circles of light dancing out from the crown.

Josh looks at one of the unfinished crossword puzzles. He sits on an orange crate, studying the puzzle.

"I work the crossword puzzles. The dogs eat the biscuits. Sit. Sit down, honey. If you like puzzles, go right ahead, honey. Goodness, doesn't your family take the paper?"

"We don't have a bird."

Nana laughs; her laughter spins out like tiny circles of light that are almost visible. Suddenly, a bird sings out, "Bird. Bird. Here, bird. Bird."

Nana whistles back-- "Yellow bird, hush."

"Yellow bird, hush." The Bird mimics.

Josh laughs. He glances up from the cross-word puzzle at Nana who is washing the lemons at a large sink. There's no running water. Instead, she is improvising with water poured from another plastic container.

"Shell Cottage doesn't have any water of its own, so we have to improvise?"

"We?"

"Oh the dogs and I. We sneak over to Palm Cottage and borrow some water. It's on the National Register of Historic Places, but this cottage was an after-thought. Built sometime after the Browns entertained all those fancy movie stars. Oh, they still have lovely parties up at Palm Cottage. Big fancy affairs and oh my goodness, honey, you should see the wild concoctions of food they come up with. Shrimp and crab meat on tiny crackers; caviar and . . . the ice sculptures. They even had an ice sculpture of a dolphin. The dogs and I just take what's left out in the kitchen; sometimes we take it over to the Immokalee Children's Home. No sense all that pretty food feeding the ants."

Nana rolls back her sleeves and begins squeezing the juice out of the lemon. She adds a dash of sugar to a glass of water and stirs, whistling along with Yellow Bird. Then, she offers the glass of fresh lemonade to Josh, "Cheers, honey."

Josh sips the drink. It is absolutely the most delicious lemonade he has ever tasted. Not too sweet. Just a little tart, enough to make his lips pucker but the juice tingles and tickles. He gulps it down. His eyes pop open-- "Wow."

"Goodness, honey. haven't you ever had lemonade?"

"Only the kind that comes in a box. My sister sells it outside our house for fifty cents."

"Yes, I've had some. It's delicious."

"You bought Chelsea's lemonade?"

"Of course, I always buy lemonade from children. Now, where is that mushroom?"

Nana sifts through the curious fruits and potions inside a small refrigerator and takes out a glass jar. "Ah, I forgot I hid it behind the dog biscuits. I'm getting to be quite a good hider."

Josh considers asking who she's hiding things from but he can't because he's absolutely fascinated by the concoction growing, or brewing or simmering inside the jar. It's almost scary. Like a live spider, spinning its web inside a mixture of seaweed and mud. Caramel colored water slushes around the mushroom. "What is that?"

Nana sips from the jar. Smacks her lips and lets out a blissful "Ah... Kabusha Tea. An ancient secret. This mushroom was a gift from an old friend. The mushrooms grow in the sacred mountains of Tibet. Keeps you young." She closes her eyes, takes several long sips, shivers and offers the jar to wide-eyed Josh who refuses,

"No thanks. If I get any younger I won't get to stay up past eight. I'll just stick to the lemonade."

He winks. She winks. They click their glasses. "Here's to the pies." There's a breath, a moment of silence between new friends.

"Nana, what are you going to do with the pies?"

"Why, sell them, of course, at the Saturday Morning Market and buy a present for our Angel." She closes the lid on the jar, places the medicinal mushroom drink back in the frig and turns to the lemons.

"What angel?" Josh finishes off the lemonade and considers asking for more but changes his mind. Above the sink, a dozen or more glass angels catch the light, creating a prism of color that illumines the lemons. He turns the orange crate to face the sink, listening.

"You've probably seen the big Christmas Tree in Old Naples, in front of Tony's Off Third?"

"Sure."

"Well, the Salvation Army places paper angels on the tree and on each angel there's a child's name with a special wish for Christmas. When you bring back a gift, you get to exchange a paper angel for one that's crystal. And when all the angels are hung back on the tree, on Christmas eve, it lights up, just like a thousand fireflies sizzling in the dusk."

She takes down a small glass angel hanging in the window and hands it to Josh. "Here." Then, for the first time, she notices the candy cane in the empty soup pot. "Why who on earth . . . ? Someone came for soup and pie, Josh. And left us a candy cane."

Josh, however, is not listening. He turns the small angel over in his hand, "It's not crystal. It's glass." The angel slips through his fingers and hits the floor, breaking a wing. Nana, distracted by the stranger's gift of the candy cane, doesn't notice. Josh quickly scoops up the broken angel, hangs it back up in the window and stuffs the broken wing into his pocket.

"Well, I hope our traveler enjoyed the soup. Quite polite, I think, to leave a present. Now, shall we squeeze those lemons?" Nana rolls up her sleeves, slips into an apron and begins washing a very large, pale yellow lemon.

Josh stands, feeling small and embarrassed. He glances back out through the screen door, "Nana, I can only stay for a little while."

"Well of course, a young man like you has very important things to do. It has been a pleasure to meet you, Josh."

He hesitates, looks back down at the crossword puzzle, finishes a word and hands her the paper, "Seven down and five across. Tennebrae."

"Yes, of course. 'Shadows before the dawn.'" Nana places the washed lemon onto a soft linen towel, then picks up another. There is a moment; a breath of stillness inside the cottage. Josh turns towards the door, but doesn't leave. It is as if he is waiting, wondering whether to tell Nana about the angel. He watches her clean and then begin peeling off the rind, grating it into small pieces. There is something almost sacred about the making of the lemon pie. She muses, whistles softly to herself, aware of his presence but not pushing him to stay or leave. Then, as if talking to the angels that hang like wind chimes in the window, she says, "The secret of course is in the rind. Little bits of rind go right into the pie. The Shakers knew just the right balance between sweet and tart."

"Miss Hawkins, I mean Nana ..." Josh steps closer in, wrinkling the small place in his forehead that has been wrinkled before, and he speaks slowly, "There wasn't any snipe, was there?"

Nana squeezes a lemon, listening without looking at him, "Hm-m-m."

"You just didn't want me to get hurt, did you, up on the Ferris Wheel. But I wasn't going to ... I go up there lots. I like the way the wind feels up there, the way it whips against you. And the way it feels to let loose of everything, swing far out and fly. But I wouldn't do anything crazy."

She puts down the lemon and wipes her face. "You get lonely sometimes, eh?"

"Not really. I've got Chelsea and Baby Ghost--he's around even when you think he's not. And Chad. Mom and Dad are usually somewhere ... in the house. Not fighting, but silent. Kind of silent with each other." Josh stuffs his hand into his pocket and feels the sharp edge of the broken wing. He winces. And somehow the pain makes it easier to tell the truth, "Yeah. Sometimes. Don't you?"

She hands him a lemon, "No, not since I took off my shoes."

He finishes peeling off the rind, "I don't understand."

"If I ever get just a twinge of feeling lonely, I go outside and I walk in the grass, or the warm sand or some times I go down to the Gulf and just stand in the water, letting it tickle my feet. And you know what, Josh, I caught on to a secret. You can't be lonely."

"I don't think that would work for me. My dad's pretty big on always wearing shoes. He's afraid we'll step on a nail or . . ."

"Well, I don't go barefoot in the street." She looks at him with that same knowing kind of look. "It's a different kind of barefoot--it's going barefoot with the soul."

He finishes peeling the lemon; the rind curls into yellow ribbons that fall onto the cutting board. Josh looks up at her through his long bangs, "I gotta go." He opens the screen door, turns around, "There's no such thing as a snipe."

Nana stops peeling the lemon, glances up, "I can't tell you whether snipe are real anymore than I could say whether there's a real Santa Claus. But to live in a world believing only in things that you can see, well, Josh, that's like living in tennebrae, the shadows of life and never waking up to the dawn." She offers him a lemon, palm-flat.

He takes it, not knowing why. She smiles, "For the lemonade stand. Tell Chelsea to use real lemons."

The screen door bangs shut behind him. Nana whistles, then calls out, "Come to the Market, Josh. Six o'clock."

He's half-way across the yard, past the flamingos, "What for?"

"To help sell the pies, of course."

Then, the screen door closes and Nana Hawkins disappears. Josh tosses the lemon over his head, catches it and heads for the Banyan Tree. As he pulls himself up into its smooth branches, Josh remembers his bike. He jumps down, picks up the bike and heads back down the path towards the alley.

This time, he notices the yellow butterfly perched in the tall fichus hedge. He slips through the portal, climbs onto his bike and takes off, pedaling barefoot towards the distant Gulf.

CHAPTER TWELVE

As the alley disappears behind him, Josh stands up on the bike. Facing the wind, whipping off the Gulf, he glides, a solitary, winged soul. Barefoot. In the distance, behind a row of Royal Palm Trees, he catches the outline of the Pier. It rises up out of the sea, yawning into a thin line where the sky and water melt together. Iridescent and curiously, abandoned of human life. And there is no sense of form but rather light, reflecting out in all directions. And even beyond the secret portal leading into the abandoned orchard and Shell Cottage, Josh can still feel her presence. Nana has shown him a different way of seeing--seeing not with the eyes, but with the heart.

Then, suddenly Palm Cottage appears. Behind the white picket fence, sitting alone, sheltered by palms and the out-stretched, walking shoots of the Banyan Tree, the historic cottage whispers "Secrets." And Josh knows the secret. Behind the Banyan Tree, behind the old Palm Cottage, a fascinating human spirit weaves her spell of good deeds and noble intentions. Painting the old guest house with trailing wildflowers (all of which she knows by name), decorating the trim with seashells collected from the beach at dawn, showing kindness to dogs and strangers alike -- Nana Hawkins. He closes his eyes and sees her face.

Suddenly, he opens his eyes. Palm Cottage appears as it has always been. A simple cottage with a wide, screened front porch. A sidewalk. A garden. Closed for the Season. He glances up at the Historic Marker and for the first in a long, long time, Josh stops and reads the sign, "Second Oldest Residence in Naples. Home of

Lawrence and Alexandra Brown. They entertained lavishly. Heddy Lamar, Montgomery Cliff stayed here."

Then, a voice calls out from the Banyan Tree-- "Josh!"

Josh walks his bike up closer to the tree where Chelsea is dangling upside down from a branch, waving a wand. Her eyes are shut tight.

"Hey Chels! Chelsea--what are you doing?"

"Is she gone yet?"

"Who?"

"The Wicked Ugly Smelly Old Witch of the 'We Care About Kids Sitters Service'. Ugh."

Josh grabs her toes, tickling her. "I doubt it."

Chelsea giggles, closes her eyes and waves the wand. "Maybe I forgot something. I'll try a different spell."

"Come on, get down. I'll go check on Chad." He starts across the street. Chelsea swings right-side up, calling after him.

"Wait, Josh, are you hungry? Look!"

Josh turns around; Chelsea is scrambling back down the tree, disappears into the trunk and reappears, holding out a frothy meringue topped lemon pie. There's a piece missing.

"Where'd you get that?"

"Here. The Banyan Tree, of course. You should taste it. It has real lemon bits inside."

Josh shakes his head, "Well that is some Banyan Tree. Keep working on that spell, Chels." He waves a quick good-bye and heads out into the street. He hears the phone just as he reaches the porch and takes the steps with a quick burst of energy. As the door bangs shut behind him, Josh dives for the phone, narrowly missing a snoring Clara Upslovsky. The Russian babysitter is now decorated with colorful balloons tied to her chair. She snores with a sort of backwards gulp of air that she releases in small spitting coughs. Josh picks up the receiver--

"Hello. Oh, hey ..."

"Hello. Josh, it's mom." Dee's bright voice bubbles into the room.

Josh scoots down onto the floor, trying to get as far away from the snoring Upslovsky as possible, "Mom. Hi."

Mrs. Upslovsky burps.

"Josh, what was that?"

"Oh, Chad has the T.V. on." He sounds very convincing; then, out of the corner of his eye, he spots Chocolate Chip, the hamster, darting over to Upslovsky. His little paws get stuck in honey, dripping down from the chair. The hamster begins to lick Upslovsky's toes. She giggles in her blissful, burping sleep.

Dee's voice cuts in--"Where is everybody, Josh? I've been calling all afternoon. Are you all right? Where's Mrs. Upsl . . . whatever her name is?" There's a lightness in her voice.

"Oh yeah, well, we're fine. Great. Fantastic. Really. She's . . . Mrs. Upslovsky's taking a nap."

"Really? What time is it -- isn't it supper time? Did she find the casserole?"

"We ate early."

"How's Chad--still mad at Warfield?"

Josh tries to kick Chocolate Chip away from Mrs. Upslovsky's toes. He drops the phone. Makes a quick recovery, "Mom, are you still there? Sorry. I dropped the phone. Chad's fine. He's outside playing basketball. And Chelsea . . ."

"I'd like to talk to Chelsea."

"Oh mom, she's eating a popsicle. She's outside. Playing with Upslovsky."

"I thought you said Mrs. Upslovsky was taking a nap."

"Oh, well, she woke up. Kind of. Listen, I've got to go. Chelsea's fine. She's eating a pie she found in the Banyan Tree."

"Josh, wait. What's going on?"

"Nothing. Just, Chocolate Chip escaped."

"Oh. Is that all? Well, put some food and water out and his cage. He'll come back."

"Yeah. Sure. Have you found a house yet?"

"Not yet. Josh, you've got our number. Call us or if you need anything, go next door to the neighbors."

The hamster climbs up Upslovsky's legs. The woman is dripping in honey. Chocolate Chip is in hamster heaven. He licks her hands, licks her belly, climbs up her chest, up her face and sits on top of her head. Her hair is sprayed; it's like a nest. Mrs. Upslovsky opens one eye; she raises one hand and feels the top of her head--

Josh motions to the hamster to "get down"; and whispers into the phone, "Mom, I've got to go."

"I love you, honey." Dee's voice trails off. Mrs. Upslovsky feels the furry hamster and screams. The hamster rolls over onto his back, sticks all four feet up into the air and opens his little mouth and disappears into Mrs. Upslovsky's hair.

Seconds later, the Russian babysitter passes out. Josh scoots over to her chair and looks for the hamster. But Chocolate Chip has escaped.

CHAPTER THIRTEEN

"Br--rring!"

The trill of the phone startles Cape out of his elfin-nap; he reaches in his pocket and pulls out the cell, "Hello? Caperton Elf, here."

"Cape, you forgot to call. Peppermint Palm, remember, buddy, what's happening?" Jingles voice sounds smooth and a little too charming; in the background, Cape hears giggles from the Barbie Dolls and Elvis singing 'Blue Christmas." He catches Blitzen's eye and holds out the receiver so that the reindeer can hear the commotion. Blitz rolls his eyes and snorts.

"Oh right, Jingles. Well, Peppermint Palm wasn't home. Or, she was, but she was taking a nap. I think she's probably a 'no' but, there was another little Cottage, with all these seashells and painted flowers and some greyhounds and a window with soup. Jingles, you have got to taste this soup."

Jingles cuts in, "Greyhounds? Soup? What are you talking about?" There's more Barbie Doll giggles and Cape catches on that he's on a speaker phone.

"Jingles, am I talking to you or the Barbies?"

"Sorry, Cape. I'm going have to handle this. Just hold on." Cape again holds out the receiver and both he and Blitzen get an earful--

"Santa, big guy, don't think of it as exercise. It's more like energy enhancement. You get vibrating at an incredible speed and you're going to attract the same kind of energy--candy canes for candy canes. Bad analogy. Jingle Bells for jingle bells. There's this incredible field of energy all around you, right. And you're going to put into that field, into your own powerful aura just the tiniest little desire— a different picture of yourself. And wow, you're going to manifest your destiny by feeling, really feeling thin. Okay, I lost you. Now, just watch the Barbies. Come on girls, lets' take it from the top. A little more of that . . . you got it. Yeah. Great. You're lookin' good, Santa." Then, the giggles, music and Santa's groans disappear and Jingles is back on the phone with Cape. "Sorry about that. I'm coaching the Barbies to get Santa to try a little belly dancing. Now, what's this about Peppermint Palm?"

"Blitzen and I think we should consider whoever lives back of the Banyan Tree. The place had a very strong energy. Very, I don't know, peaceful. And an essence that was pure spirit. And the greyhounds, gentle whispers with luminous skin and eyes . . with looks that would melt your heart."

"You want Santa to marry a dog? Get with the program, Cape."

"I'm with the program, Jingles. I just think we may have dashed into this without considering . . . well, you know, I think we're looking for a Nine."

"Nine!! We're going for a ten."

"I'm not talking about physical features; I'm considering the exact match on the Enneagram. Now if Santa is a fun-loving Seven, then I think what we want is a Nine. Nine's are old souls. Peacemakers."

Jingles suddenly switches Cape off the Speaker Phone; he drops his voice-- "Cape, you're not making sense. I need you to be practical. None of this Goofy--

"Suffi . . . See, each person, each elf has their own path towards destiny. Towards wholeness and what I see for Santa is an individual who knows how to . . ."

"No. Stop thinking. Just get to Cane Run and call me. Call me!!

Just before Jingles hangs up, he yells out -- "No, No Santa. Give me that chocolate bell. Who gave Santa the chocolate bell?" Then, he hangs up.

Cape shakes his head, "I don't see Santa belly dancing, do you, Blitz? Well, where's that letter?" Cape ruffles through a sack, tossing out pistachios and finds the letter. It's written on a torn piece of notebook paper.

CHAPTER FOURTEEN

Cape tucks the cell phone back into a stocking and cracks a pistachio, "Jingles isn't into the Enneagram." He tosses a shell back over his head and Blitzen snorts, "What, what did I do? How can you litter up here? And pistachio shells aren't really litter? They're bio--they're digestible. He cracks open a handful, then shoots up. "What about handwriting." With a sudden burst of energy, he takes out a shimmering magnifying glass and muses over the sheet of notebook paper.

"I learned this trick from a wise old elf. He was a nine on the Enneagram. Humph." Cape muses aloud to Blitzen, who has little interest in handwriting for obvious reasons. "Blitz, the slant looks like whoever wrote this responds pretty quickly to their emotions and the dot on the "i" is a sign of loyalty. The t's are crossed really high--maybe a dreamer here. But there's a stubborn mark in the t and y's look like not a whole lot of folks are going to get real close. But the o's wide open, she'll say whatever comes to mind. The double loop in the a bothers me,. Blitz. A little deception. How's that?"

Blitzen is looking for directions; he shakes his harness bell and snorts.

Cape folds the letter and glances at a map. "Cane Run is near Old Elkhorn Creek. Yep, and that's the Old Sinkhole. I'd bet my pistachios that's Cane Run Road. Lets' take a closer look."

The sleigh dips. Cape continues to analyze the handwriting, musing aloud--"Traits of secretiveness, maybe even-- oh!"

A wisp of wind takes the letter right out of Cape's fingers and down it falls, through snowflakes and stardust, right into a chimney. Cape quickly turns Blitz towards the ground, the sleigh circles a small house with a front porch. A string of colored lights dangle across the porch eaves and plastic poinsettias stick up out of the snow like popsicles. Curiously, there's a white stretch limo parked out-front of the house. On a mailbox, Cape reads "561 Cane Run Road."

"Lets' take her to the roof, Blitz." As the sleigh lands quietly on the house roof, Cape catches a fleeting glimpse of the letter, bobbing on warm air coming up out of the chimney. Then, suddenly, the letter nose-dives down into a waft of steamy air. Cape jumps out, chases the letter, peering down into the smoky chimney and coughs, "Talk me out of it, Blitz."

Blitzen snorts, shaking his harness bell.

"Right. Thanks. I'll just take the sensible solution and knock on the door." Cape slides down the roof, scoots down a drain pipe and lands smack dab in front of the meanest, ugliest and biggest Chihuahua ever to come out of the Pound. The dog draws back his thin lips, dripping saliva and growls. Cape drops to his knees.

"Ah-ha. A dog!"

The dog's tail sticks straight up or rather curls round, straight up. It's got some Akita in with the Chihuahua and possibly some Chow because when it opens it smooth, a black tongue rubs across the gums. Signaling trouble. Cape tries to remember what Santa said to the little mechanical dog back up at the North Pole and he slips into a sort of Irish brogue--"You're a dog, right. Yes? We don't have many of you rogues up at the North Pole. The reindeer get a bit skittish--on account of you fellows looking like wolves."

The dog goes stiff. Staring. Silently.

"Not that I think you look like a wolf."

The Chihuahua's eyes sizzle. He is going to eat the elf.

"Don't look him in the eye. Thanks, Blitz. Appreciate the advice from your safe perch on the roof. Okay, now sit. Sit."

Miraculously, the dog sits.

"He sat. Great Jingles, you sat. Good. Good little dog. Shake hands."

The Chihuahua-chow-Akita mix sticks out a paw. Cape shakes the dog's paw.

"Yes, nice to meet you." Cape keeps shaking the dog's paw, turns his head and glances through a window which has been completely taken out by a phone which now lies just beneath the windowsill in the soft ferns. The little house is bulging at the seams with Christmas decorations. A tinsel tree with blinking blue lights turns in circles, playing a tinny sounding "Jingle Bell Rock".

Inside 561 Cane Run Road, Gerald Dean sits, blowing bubbles, sticking the gum to his nose and watching bug-eyed while the family gathers to trim the tree. One more star or candy cane-and the shiny blue tinsel tree will ignite. Gerald Dean offers a stick of gum to Pumpkin, a sweet-faced, pudgy sixteen year old, pacing the floor. He's dressed in a tux, holding a drooping corsage and every now and then, he knocks on a closed bathroom door. Behind him, staring out the front window, mumbling to herself, is Mildred, an ancient curmudgeon. And on a tired mustard-yellow and brown sofa sits middle-age, worn down and tired out Mable fanning her face with a fan advertising the Milward Funeral Home. She's drinking a soda pop which occasionally she slushes around her mouth. Lulu May, in her early twenties, is perming Mable's hair while also nursing a sleeping baby.

Occasionally, someone hangs a candy cane on the tree. Carolyn Ramey, dressed in a Winnie the Pooh t-shirt that reads, "Squeezed Fresh Daily" raps hard on the closed door. She succeeds in cracking open the door, then it bangs shut in her face and there's the sound of a lock popping. "Chiquita Lynn open this door, baby! Pumpkin has done gone and rented a limousine and bought you a corsage and made reservations at the Cracker Barrel and ain't nobody gonna be lookin' at your hair, baby."

Loud sobs pierce the tinny sound of the twirling Christmas tree now playing its second Greatest Christmas Hits of the Fifties, Sixties and Seventies, "Grandma Got Run Over by A Reindeer."

Pumpkin, looking pitiful, shakes his head, "Please Chiquita Lynn, lets' just go to the prom."

"Mildred's got to take a bath, Chiquita." Carolyn pours some coffee into the base of the fake Christmas tree--looking at Mildred who sticks out her tongue. Mildred picks up a coloring book and begins coloring all the while eyeing the front door. She glimpses Cape, growls, "I ain't taking no bath."

Carolyn tries to turn the knob on the bathroom door, steps back, "Pumpkin, you try."

Cape watches all this through the open screen door, debating whether to risk the Chihuahua or take a chance on getting kissed by Mildred (who is now batting her lash less eyes at him and blowing kisses.)

Suddenly, the phone rings. Mable answers and catches on that she can't talk without her teeth. She points to a small tin container, motioning to skinny Gerald Dean who prefers to be invisible; he scoots over towards the door, shaking his buzzed head, "Not me. I ain't touching your teeth."

Carolyn takes the phone, "Hello." Her voice, low, relaxed, betrays nothing of the chaos circling around her. She motions to Mable, "Mable, get your teeth." Then, she speaks into the receiver, "Oh hello, Moo, is Peaches over there? No, they ain't gone yet. Chiquita got her hair fixed, now she says she ain't going. She don't like the way they fixed it and she paid . . . " Carolyn holds out the phone for a second, "Chiquita, what'd you pay baby?"

Sobs, louder, rising several octaves, escape from behind the bathroom door. Carolyn continues talking to Moo and catches Mildred trying to sneak out the front door, Uh-uh Mildred, you ain't going nowhere. Sit down. Color. I got your Lottery Tickets. Pumpkin, here, it's your mama on the phone." Carolyn hands the phone to Pumpkin who sinks down onto a chair; his face puckers up-

"Hello, Mama. I guess we ain't going to make it to the Cracker Barrel. Tell Charlene and Billy Bob to go on without us."

More sobs swim into the room, drowning out the Christmas tree, playing Hit Number Three, a tinny rendition of the classic Jingle Bells (in Spanish.) Carolyn looks at the door, shakes her head, "Same soup warmed over", then disappears back into the kitchen. Mildred seizes the moment to sneak out the front door. She sees Cape pointing like a beagle, crouched on the ground, near a cactus. He speaks, "Ah, Merry Christmas, ma'am."

Mildred looks at Cape, at his ears, "I ain't taking no bath. King!" She swoops up the snarling Chihuahua and takes off. Seconds later, Cape sees King, with a snarl frozen on this lips, stick his head out of the limo sunroof, eyeing Cape. Cape smiles, waving "Bye bye." The elf stands, shakes and knocks on the door, which is about half-open. Suddenly the door swings wide open and lets in a rush of air. Pumpkin turns, sees Cape and mistaking him for the limo driver, pulls out a crumpled twenty dollar bill, "Man, I'm sorry. My girlfriend's stuck in the bathroom and she ain't coming out. I guess we won't be needing the limo."

More sobs. Mable and Lulu May turn up the television, trying to drown out the rising floodwater of sighs, tears and wails. Carolyn reappears with a coffee pot and pours Mable and Lulu May some coffee. "Hello, I've picked the lock before but my eyes is going. Here, you try." She puts down the coffee pot by the steamy perm solution. Cape smiles uneasily, "Oh well, I'm not really very good at these sort of ... "

Carolyn peeks through the keyhole, "Chiquita, you still in there?"

Sobs. Mable turns up the T.V. and Lulu May dips her sponge in the coffee pot and drips hot coffee on Marigold's rollers. Neither notices because the T.V. show is parading bikini-clad beauties in front of a rich bachelor. Carolyn motions to Cape and he tip-toes closer to the door. He leans down and peeks through the keyhole at Chiquita Lynn, a striking sixteen year old African American girl, sobbing her heart out. She's wearing a red sequin dress. Her shining black hair is pulled up in tight ringlets with a stray wisp stuck to her forehead like a third eye with a tail. She leans down and spits into the keyhole. Cape shoots straight up. For a second, his little elfin feet actually leave the floor and he does a small spin before landing. This acrobatic trick gets the baby's attention who oos and ahhs, giggling at Cape who bows.

Carolyn picks up the coffee pot and starts to retreat back into the kitchen, "Luly May, you got coffee dripping out of one of Mable's curlers. Chiquita Lynn, you ought to be ashamed of yourself."

The sobs stop. Chiquita speaks--"Granny, I am not coming out."

Suddenly, as if dared, Carolyn pulls Cape over to the door. "Push."

As Cape and Carolyn push hard, the door suddenly breezes open and out prances Chiquita, all decked out for the prom. For a second, everyone in the room freezes. Even the singing tree takes a breath.

"Granny . . ." Sob. "I'm so . . ."

"Ugly." Gerald Dean, eating a banana by the T.V. stares at her, "Chiquita, you sure got the uglies."

Carolyn shoots him a look Chiquita stares at him, her eyes pop. Swallowing self-pity, she tries to retreat back into the bathroom. But Cape sticks out his arm and links it around the desperate girl's waist. "If I may say so, I have never seen anyone more exquisite. Like a Monarch Butterfly in sequins."

Gerald Dean puts one finger in his mouth (as if about to throw-up) and stares out the window where he sees the limo driving off. He jumps up, "Excuse me, but Mildred stole your limo."

Chiquita starts to shake. The sequins shiver. Her gold loop earrings spin wildly. Gerald Dean back ups, staring, "Watch out, mister. She's going blow."

The phone rings again and Carolyn grabs it, "Hello." She motions for Gerald Dean to hush and softens her voice, "Hello."

Gerald Dean tugs at Cape's sleeve, "I'll bet it's the police. Mildred's always getting picked up by the police. "Ya hungry?"

Gerald Dean breaks off some of his banana, then picks up Lulu May's bowl of popcorn, down to kernels.

Cape shakes his head, sniffing the air, "Is something burning?"

Gerald Dean glances at Mable's hair. The perm is steaming. Beads of perspiration dot Mable's face but she and Lulu May are glued to the Bachelorettes now boo-hooing over rejections from the swarthy bachelor. Gerald Dean flings down the popcorn bowl, "Granny, Lulu May has done fried Mable's hair."

There's a loud knock on the screen door. Carolyn, still on the phone shouts, "Come in."

Gerald Dean opens the door and lets in a charming man in a ponytail, licking an ice cream cone. He has Mildred by the arms; she's all smiles. He speaks, "Look, does somebody here want to go to a prom because I got this limo ..." He sees Carolyn and tips his chauffeur's hat, "Oh, hello."

Everyone stares at Mildred, patting the driver's arm, "Marshall. Marshall."

Carolyn dismisses whoever's on the other end of the phone, "Never mind. Some man just showed up with Mildred." She hangs up.

Mildred tightens her grasp on the man's arm, "I ain't taking no bath."

Carolyn offers the driver a paper napkin for the dripping ice cream. He takes it, tips his hat again, "Thank you. Sorry."

Then Carolyn glances at Cape, back at the limo driver and back at Cape, "Wait a minute, if he's the limo driver, who are you?"

Cape bows, "Caperton Elf. Hello, sir, Merry Christmas." He shakes hands with the limo driver.

"What? Oh, Elvis Whitley. Well, look, sorry about the mix-up, Caperton. She got in and said for me to take her home. I said, 'Okay, but what about the prom. She said the prom was off because somebody burned Chiquita's hair and so I said, 'Where's home, little lady?' And she says, 'Parkers Mill, down by the river.' So, we drove down there and there's nothin' there, 'ceptin' for the airport."

Chiquita hands Carolyn a brush, holds a mirror up to her face. Carolyn brushes the teary-eyed girl's hair. It's been sprayed pretty thick with hair spray so the brush sticks a couple of times, "Sit down."

Chiquita, Cape and the Limo Driver (and the snarling Chihuahua King) all sit down at the exact same time. The Limo Driver licks the dripping ice cream cone, continuing with his story, "So, I said, 'Maybe we got the wrong address' and she says her daddy would know. Well, I looked at her and she's got to be -- what, eighty?"

"Hold still." the brush sticks to Chiquita's hair. Carolyn grabs hold of her shoulder and gives it a good yank.

"Ouch, granny!" Chiquita pops some juicy fruit in her sweet lips, chews, blows and sulks.

Carolyn looks at the limo driver, "Mildred will be seventy-five on Christmas day."

Cape smiles, "Happy Birthday, Mildred."

Mildred bats her lash less eyes and winks. The limo driver keeps on with his story, "And so, I say to myself, 'Elvis, go figure, the little lady's eighty; daddy must be a hundred and ...'"

"Dead." Carolyn holds up the mirror. "You look pretty, baby. Unstick that curl." She licks her finger and dabs the curl on Chiquita forehead, "There. Now, go have a good time." Carolyn scoots Chiquita over to Pumpkin who scrambles to his feet--"Go. Git on out of here." Then, she turns to Elvis, "Well, what do I owe you for taking Mildred to the river and getting the ice cream?" She opens a huge bag, rummages for coins.

Elvis licks the cone faster and faster; it's melting really fast. "Forget it. It's Christmas." He looks over at Pumpkin, "You two still want to go to that Prom?"

Pumpkin beams. Chiquita prances out the door. As the limo driver goes out, he tosses the ice cream cone to King who eats it in one gulp, licks his lips and snarls at Cape--

Gerald Dean whispers to Cape, "Don't worry. He's just like Mable-ain't got no teeth on account of the pop."

Carolyn shuts the door behind the happy couple and turns to Cape, "So, if you're not the limo driver ..."

Cape sticks out his hand, "Caperton Elf."

Carolyn isn't impressed, "I heard you the first time, Elf."

Cape goes up on tip-toe and slides over to the fireplace. There isn't a fire, The steam must have come from the perm solution. He leans down and picks up the torn notebook paper-- "Here, your letter?" (Carolyn looks blank.) "'Lovin', Lookin' or Leavin'?"

A sheepish Gerald Dean nose-dives for the sagging couch. Carolyn takes the letter and rolls her tongue, shooting a look at the boy.

Cape steps forward, "Yes, your letter says that you love kids, love to cook ..."

From under the couch, a small muffled voice speaks "Granny cooks as good as the Cracker Barrel."

Carolyn mumbles, "Humph!" She pours a cup of coffee for Cape; pops open a soda and takes a long swallow, "So, Mr. Elf, let me get this straight. You're here to see if maybe I could come cook for .. what'd you say his name is?"

"Oh no, Ms. Ramey. Not just cook but also ..."

"Clean?"

"That's not necessary. The elves .."

"He has elves?" Carolyn sips the soda. Catching on. She thinks.

"We're looking for a Mrs. Santa Claus. A wife."

Mable looks up from her rollers, so tight they make her eyebrows wrinkle. "Carolyn don't even like Christmas. Says she ain't got the spirit."

Mildred looks up, "Well, she can't have mine."

Lulu May starts smiling kind of funny-like, looking around, "Are we on some kind of weird T.V, show, you know with the hidden cameras cuz I'm nursing a baby here." She covers her blouse over the baby's sweet face. Lulu May picks up a brush and starts fixing her hair and reties the pink yarn in the baby's one and only strand of hair.

There's a loud knock on the door. This time, everyone says, "Come in."

Cape is very distressed, "This isn't a joke."

Carolyn places some cookies on a plate, covers it with a napkin and speaks very slowly to Cape--as if she too suspects that she's being taped, "Here, Mr. Elf, take these. Fresh baked."

Cape's ears start to wiggle. "I'm not here for cookies."

Carolyn nods, speaking very slowly, "Mr. Elf, do you have any idea how many kids and old people live in this house, not to mention deaf dogs?"

"He's deaf?" Cape shoots his hands up over his own ears which are about to take off. He takes a small bite of the offered cookie, "No ma'am."

"Seventeen, counting Mildred who doesn't eat or sleep except sitting up. You expect me to just get up and walk out. "Lovin', Lookin' or Leavin"--humph! It's the same soup warmed over but I'm the one's got to dish it up, serve it hot and make sure nobody, nobody goes to bed a'hungry. Tell me something, Mr. Elf, who's going to look out for all these old people, deaf dogs and children if I fly off to the North Pole?" She starts to freshen Cape's cup; he places his hand over the top--

"I'm not really a coffee drinker."

"No, didn't think so. How about some milk?"

Suddenly, the limo driver pokes his head inside-- "Lottery tickets, Ms. Ramey. Found them on the back seat." He hands the tickets to Mildred.

Carolyn holds out the plate of cookies, "Mr. Whitley, you got a heart as big as heaven. Let me fix you a cup of coffee. You take it black?"

Elvis tips his hat to Mildred who is blowing him kisses, murmuring "Marshal, Marshal." Elvis puts down the tickets and grins at Carolyn, "Little cream. Toss in one of those cookies--what are these?" He takes a huge bite.

"Hermit Cookies. Oatmeal raisins with mouse droppings." Carolyn fills a Styrofoam cup with coffee and hands it to Elvis. "Here. Have another."

" . . . um-m delicious." He swallows the cookie whole. "You are one lovely lady, Ms. Ramey, and you've got a lovely family and a lovely Christmas tree." The singing tree is stuck; it's been playing the same tune over and over.

Carolyn nods, "Same soup warmed over." She gives the tree a little nudge and it spins round, singing "You better watch out. You better not pout."

Elvis takes a couple more cookies wrapped up in a napkin and goes out. Carolyn takes the coffee pot back into the kitchen. Cape glances at the lottery tickets lying on Mildred's lap. Mildred is staring at the television set, half-snoring. Cape takes out the velvet bag and sprinkles some Christmas Cheer on the tickets. Mildred's eyes shoot open; he puts a finger up against his lips, whispering, "Take that bath, Mildred. It's Christmas."

Cape slips a cookie under the couch to Gerald Dean and goes outside. Suddenly, as the screen door closes behind the elf, a mischievous wind whips through the room. The lights blink and go off. Carolyn comes into the living room with a glass of milk--looks around, "Mr. Elf?"

The power comes back on, but the television has gone off and a small radio is now playing. Pippa's voice comes in on the radio.

"Hello all you lucky Florida Lottery players. The Jackpot is forty million. Wow! And our winning numbers are. .."

As Pippa announces the lottery numbers, Cape slips back up onto the roof. He sits in the sleigh, nibbling the cookies. Blitz cracks his neck, eyeing the cookie and Cape tosses him a small bite. Then, he tosses the reindeer a great big cookie and clicks the reins. Blitzen swallows the delicious cookie and flies. From below, out of the chimney of 561 Cane Run Road, a great cry rises up--"Alleluia. Mildred done won the lottery."

Mildred's voice cracks a dry reply, "Well, I still ain't taking no bath."

Gerald Dean flies out onto the front porch, waving his arms over his head, whistling to Cape, "Merry Christmas! MERRY CHRISTMAS!"

Cape leans over the side of the sleigh, "Gerald Dean--

"Huh?" The boy stares up at the flying reindeer and sleigh.

"Don't forget the cookies for Santa."

The sleigh nose-dives into luminous star-dust. Cape's voice disappears into the sounds of celebration coming from inside the little brown brick house with the Chihuahua (smacking his lips, gumming a candy cane) peacefully sitting on the crooked front porch.

Cape, all smiles, takes out the cell phone, "Jingles, yo. This is Cape. Great Cookies. But she's committed. Who's on second?" He pops his short legs up onto the side of the sleigh, enjoying the delicious cookie. He pokes his finger into the dough, pulls out tiny dark piece inside the cookie, "Hey Blitz, did she say mouse droppings?"

The reindeer snorts.

"No. You don't think." He hesitates. Risks it. Takes a bite. Relieved, he swallows the chocolate chip.

Jingles' voice comes in loud and clear over the cell-phone, "Cape. Save the cookies. I'm starving. We've got Santa on Slim Fast, Adkins and the Perricone Prescription. Light on Carbs. Big on Salmon." There's some static; he switches to the speaker and yells, "One more lap."

Cape finishes the cookie, "I think she thought I was with some television show. Candid Camera or something."

Jingles sounds distracted, "Hit the mat. Fifty crunches. A hundred leg lifts. Pull up that belly, stick it in, say 'Ah-ah-' as you breathe out. Tuck the gut, Santa."

Cape taps the phone receiver, "Jingles, take it easy on him. You can't melt a century of cocoa and marzipan in a single day."

Jingles isn't listening. ". . . five, six, seven. Exhale. Okay, sorry Cape. So, what about Carolyn. No show? A no go."

"Too many obligations, Jingles. Her grandson, Gerald Dean, wrote the letter."

"Oh well, what about Sugar St. Clair--the Royal Poinsettia Ball. But remember Cape, dont twitch the ears."

There's some static on the cell phone. Jingles talks louder. "Cape. Caperton. The ears. Remember, don't twitch."

Jingles' voice fades out. The sleigh dips, then rises towards a fingernail moon as the cell phone curiously picks up radio waves. Pippa's voice comes from out of a distant star-

"So snowbirds, somewhere out there a warm-hearted lady is waiting to be Mrs. Santa Claus. Till you find her, Kris Kringle, here's to 'Lovin', Lookin' or Leavin'."

A shooting star sizzles in a downard spiral straight towards the rooftop of 561 Cane Run Road. Narrowly missing Blitzen's antler, the star glows bright, then disappears in a poof of golden light.

CHAPTER FIFTEEN

Josh hits his alarm clock shaped like Chanticleer cockle-doodling the time. Eight o'clock. Hurriedly, he dresses, gives a kick to the basketball shorts and basketball that lie smack in the middle of the floor-next to the wet towel, exactly where Chad dropped them the night before. Chad, snoring, one arm wrapped around a well-loved sock monkey, lies in a sleeping bag. At the foot of Josh's bed, a doll's head sticks out of the bed-covers. Josh hesitates, then quietly pulls back the covers, allowing the sleeping Chelsea to breathe. She opens her eyes--

"Where's my purse?"

Josh picks up the plastic pink purse, lying on the floor and tucks it in beside the doll. He starts to sit down, "Chels, I'm going over to the Market. Chad's going to take you to the Nature Conservancy." He catches on that she's gone back to sleep. As he opens the bedroom door, he hesitates, scribbles a note on a chalkboard and takes off.

Half-way down the stairs, he hears her. Mrs. Upslovsky, snoring. Nor really a human sort of snoring, more like a swarm of yellow jackets storming a helpless sticky, oozy honey hive. He glances towards the chair. Yep, she's still there. Snoozing in the yellow chair. her legs propped up, her jaw open. There's no sign of the hamster, just hamster droppings sprinkled in Mrs. Upslovsky's hairnet. Josh says, "Good morning, Mrs. Upslovsky. (real slow) "I'm going to the Market to help sell pies."

Mrs. Upslovsky's mouth quivers; parts, sputters. Her tongue picks at a piece of something stringy, stuck in her tooth. But she says nothing. Her fingers move to the television remote and for an instant, Josh freezes. Waiting. Wondering if she's going to turn on the TV and wake herself up . . . but she doesn't. The fingers relax; the tongue loosens the piece of stuck food and she slips back into blissful unconsciousness.

Josh opens the screen door and steps out into the morning. Once on his bike, he spins the wheels, seizing the day. Enjoying the pulse of rising adrenalin, the thrill of an adventure. He rides in and around the bikers and joggers, already out for their Saturday morning exercise. Some off to Tony's Off Third to sit by the fountain, enjoying muffins or triple berry scones, bunny tails (thick with cream), others heading for Cove Inn (and greasy, melt in your mouth pancakes) or further north to enjoy wheat germ pancakes outside at Morning Watch. Josh waves, smiling at strangers. Something he hasn't done in a long time. He cruises down to the parking lot back of the Pub. There's already a crowd gathering to buy fresh flowers, vegetables, exotic oils, Bonzo trees, etc. from vendors lined up under the already blistering sun. Josh searches the lot for his friend, Nana.

At first he doesn't see her. He gets off his bike and walks through the Market. Pulling his baseball cap down over his shaggy hair, keeping his head down, more out of habit than anything else. He sees a turkey near a skinny Christmas palm and hears Nana's voice--

"Oh dear, that really is terrible. I'm so sorry."

There are some gobbles, coming from the turkey and then, again her voice, "Thelma, gracious. And where is Louise?" More gobbles. "No really!"

Josh hesitates, curious but not wanting to intrude. But Nana sees him and smiles, "Oh Josh, good morning."

"Is anything wrong?

"No not a thing. Now that you're here."

The turkey ruffles her feathers and gobbles, strutting off like a little old lady with a too tight perm. Josh cracks a half-smile, "Were you just talking to that turkey?"

Nana's expression changes; she drops her voice to a whisper. "It's quite dreadful. There's a new television commercial advertising you know what as the best low-fat choice and all this new-fangled talk of protein over carbs. Very scary for the birds."

Josh crinkles his eyes against the sun melting the meringue on one of the few remaining lemon pies, "I take it you don't eat meat."

"Never eat anything that can look back at you. The eyes are the windows of the . . . oh dear, there's the trolley."

The clanging, distant but distinct, sounds the approach of the Old Naples Trolley. Josh takes off his cap, brushes his hands through his hair, puzzled, "Are you--are you going somewhere?"

"Oh yes, dear. Straight-away."

"But I thought . . ."

Nana begins to fold down her large cardboard box which has served as a booth for the pies. She wraps the last remaining pie in a paper napkin. Her whole demeanor changes; she is quite intent on catching the trolley.

"But what about the pies? The, you know, the crystal angel?"

"Sold out, honey. First thing. The Market opens at six and well, our pies have a reputation. Why there wasn't a single pie left by seven. I had to save this for Dominic or it would have been snatched up too."

Josh feels a gnawing emptiness, something he hasn't felt in such a long, long time. Usually, he doesn't let himself get disappointed. He knows better.

How could he have let this happen? He scuffs his untied tennis shoe against the soft sand and gravel. He stares at Nana; her slender fingers feel beneath the box, catch the string and suddenly it crinkles into a flat piece of cardboard--like magic!

"Oh, I do hope we're not too late. And what with my ankle and all the fuss with Thelma . . . Jump on this, will you?" She takes hold of the bike and Josh jumps on the box, flattening it even more.

"Too late for what, Ms. Hawkins?"

Josh doesn't really care. He's only asking to be polite. He's already put up his guard, wishing he hadn't come. Wishing he hadn't looked forward to something as childish and silly as selling lemon pies in a market with a' lot of strangers and flies and … She's looking at him. Again. It's that look. He raises his eyes, meets her gaze,--

"… late for?"

"Josh, the first race starts in thirty minutes." She hands him the pie and takes off. Expecting Josh to follow. And of course, he does, juggling the pie, forgetting his bike. She looks back, "Oh, you can bring your bike, of course."

Josh stops, "Bring my bike where?"

"The Dog Races. Bonita Springs. The first race starts at one thirty." Nana talks while making her way through the crowd. Even with a hurt ankle, Nana Hawkins is something to be reckoned with. She seems to never tire, an enthusiastic fan of life, Josh thinks. She is always polite, stepping out of the way of little children and elderly ladies with tiny dogs wearing bows. Josh catches up with her just as the trolley reaches the parking lot. Nana waves to the driver, a big, friendly looking man with shiny black skin and a deep bullfrog voice, shouting-- "Nana Hawkins, you bring pie? Yes?" He smiles, crinkling his forehead and laughs.

Nana ties on her sun bonnet, "Oh Dominic, thank you for stopping. Can you possibly make room for a bicycle."

Dominic grins, "We make room for the Second Avenue Baptist Church--" he gestures at the "Choir" seated behind him. "We make room for de bike."

"Oh thank you." Nana turns to Josh, "Hurry."

Josh gets off his bike. He's considering saying that he isn't coming. He only came to the Market because … why, why had he come? To sell pies. He can't think. And he can't think why he can't get on the trolley. Why he can't go to the dog races. Nana raises an eyebrow, sunlight glints off her cream-christened cheeks, "It would be wonderful if you could come, but of course, if you have other plans…"

"Well, I do have plans, kind of … ."

"Oh no, you got no plans when Hawkins got a plan." Dominic's smile--all white teeth--catches Josh by surprise. Of course, he'll get on the trolley. Why not? If Mrs. Upslovsky wakes up, which isn't likely, she'll just ask about the babies, swat a couple of flies and go back to sleep. Chad's taking Chelsea to the Conservancy. He'll be back by the time his mother calls . . . Nana's flower-print skirt catches the breeze as she lifts up the bike. "Oh dear." She glances at Josh ... "Would you be so kind as to . . ."

But Dominic shakes his head, grinning and holds the bike airborne, glancing around the trolley which is packed with the Choir.

"Can you make room for a bicycle?" Nana repeats.

"For Nana Hawkins, we make room for a rhinoceros."

"Well, we don't have a rhino, just the bike. Here, jump on."

She grabs hold of the pole and swings herself up and onto the trolley. Dominic swings the bike up and over Josh' head and places it carefully behind his driver's seat. Suddenly, the bell clangs and the sign switches its destination and takes off, clamoring gracefully around Third Avenue South, heading north, gaining speed. It all happens incredibly fast.

Josh takes off his cap, letting the warm air ruffle his hair. Josh hasn't ridden the trolley since . . . he can't remember the last time. Maybe since he got his bike. The trolley offers an entirely new view on Old Naples. There are Alligators on the street corners--dressed up as ballerinas or sophisticated shoppers, with pearls and purses. Josh has never really noticed the Alligators. Now, they seem to be absolutely everywhere--giving Naples an artsy look.

The alligators disappear and an incredibly large dinosaur appears, chained outside an auction house behind Wind in the Willows. Fifth Avenue is a sea of color-posh shops and cafes, art galleries and New Age bookstores whirl by.

"Sit down. Sit." Dominic eyes Josh with his cinnamon, coffee colored eyes. Josh glances around. Nana is sitting next to the window; next to a skinny man holding a sign that reads "Second Ave. Baptist Church Choir. Josh hesitates, then squeezes in next to a plump lady who smells just like a gardenia (she's wearing one in her thickly sprayed hair.) She hands him a fan, which he takes. She fans her face, closes her eyes and hums.

Behind him, all around him, the Second Avenue Baptist Church choir fan their faces with paper fans. Perfumed and dressed up in floral colors--fuchsia, purple and hot orange--the choir members suddenly begin humming, then singing "Swing Low Sweet Chariot."

It all happens spontaneously. Suddenly, a tall skinny man with caramel-colored skin pops up and says, "The Bible says 'Make a joyful noise unto the Lord." His eyes twinkle; he moves up to Dominic- - "We sure could use a bass, Brother." And he sings "um-hmm" in between breaths.

Dominic glances in the mirror at Nana, crinkling his forehead again, "If I sing, Brother, it won't be music, brother."

"Make a joyful noise, Brother Dominic. The Lord doesn't care about how it sounds. All music is wonderful to the Lord, isn't that right brothers and sisters?"

"Well, you's the preacher, I just drive the trolley." Dominic scowls, but it's a fake scowl and the skinny choir director laughs,

"Then, brother, you clang the bell. Every time we sing "Alleluia Amen", you clang the bell."

Suddenly, the lady next to Josh swings down low, really low, way, way low and her shimmery floral blouse shakes and shivers as she starts to gyrate and shrieks-- "I seen an angel comin' over Jordon." She shoots up her arms and another woman answers, "Comin' over Jordon to carry me home."

Even Nana sings. And Josh thinks about it. He can't help it. The music is so rich, it seems to just seep right into your skin. Into your soul.

Then the skinny choir director hits a note and all the "trolley" just hums right back and then all the ruffles and the feathers and the fans start to fly as the Choir sings out " Swing Low Sweet Chariot".

The music ripples out, surging over and around Josh and Nana, taking them into his powerful hold. The preacher/choir director raps on Dominic's back each time they sing "Alleluia Amen" and Dominic clangs the bell. It is magical. And mesmerizing. And hypnotic.

The trolley is vibrating, rattling and rolling with the music of old Negro Spirituals like "There Is A Balm In Gilead" and "When The Saints Come Marching In." And as soon as one spiritual ends, someone shouts out another and the whole choir joins in. Even Nana sings. And Josh thinks about it. He can't help it. The music is so rich, it seems to just seep right into your skin. Into your soul.

And with every "Alleluia Amen", the skinny preacher taps Dominic and Dominic clangs the bell. Then, Josh notices Nana quietly unwrapping the lemon pie. She looks at Josh and winks and he catches on. Glancing at the woman next to him, singing a gutsy "Gilead", Josh says--"Pardon me, could I . . . do you have some tissue?"

The music swells around him. The perfumed lady hands Josh a box of Kleenex and while the trolley beats out "The Alleluia Chorus" with a whole lot of clangs and clapping and foot rapping, Nana and Josh pass out pieces of the pie.

Suddenly, the preacher stops-- wiping perspiration from his brow, "Brothers and sisters, we can't eat pie that ain't been blessed."

So he says a quick blessing and then smacks his lips-- "Sister, this ain't pie. This is honey from the Land of Canaan--sent from heaven by an angel. Alleluia."

The bell clangs.

The skinny preacher shoots Dominic a look.

Then, one by one, the choir members eat the pieces of pie. They close their eyes, lick their fingers and smile. Nana stands, bows.

"We're trying to raise some money for a little paper angel on the Christmas tree."

Suddenly, a big man, singing bass, takes off his hat and passes it around and quarters and nickels, dimes and pennies drop into the hat. Nana beams. Then, another round of Sweet Charity and with tears streaming down their faces, the Choir sings for their pie.

It doesn't seem possible, but the Dog Track rises up in the distance. Nana empties the money out of the hat, counts it and squeezes Josh's hand.

"Is there enough?" Josh meets her eyes.

She points to her throat, "Can't talk." Tears stream down her face. And suddenly, the trolley slows, pulling into the blistering hot parking lot outside the track entry gates.

As they climb down off the trolley, trailing the Choir, Josh and Nana wave good-bye to Dominic. "Man, its hot." Dominic brushes his palm across Josh's thin shoulder, "High five, man. 'Here comes de Lucky." He laughs. An infectious laugh that comes from the man's soul. Josh raises his hand, small and freckled, and their two hands slap high, then low. Then, the older man hands down the bike, grinning-- "Trolley comes back at four. Don't you be late."

Nana whispers, "Alleluia".

And Dominic clangs the bell. Then, the trolley jolts forward and takes off. Nana steps down onto the steaming hot asphalt, casting a glance up at the sky, "Hotter than blue blazes. Hope that rain holds off." She digs into her giant bag and exchanges the bonnet for a huge straw hat. She glances at Josh, as if sizing up his head, and he ducks-

"No way. I'm not wearing anything that comes out of that bag."

She holds out a Goofy Hat, with dangling ears and he almost changes his mind. Then, waving, she scurries off, "Oh here, honey, you can leave the bike with Marigold."

"Marigold?"

Josh expects a giant flower growing up out of the sizzling hot asphalt. He is not disappointed.

CHAPTER SIXTEEN

"Who's Marigold, Ms. Hawkins?" Josh trails Nana, now waving wildly at a woman in humongous tennis shoes, a flower print dress and pearls. She stands just inside the entrance gate, holding a white parasol over her pretty face. As she pushes back the parasol, she smiles and her whole face beams, recognizing her friend, "Ms. Hawkins, I was wondering if you'd be showing up today. They got some yellow stars." She does a strange clucking sound, like a duck and Josh almost swallows his gum. Marigold looks like a duck.

But Nana wasn't laughing in the least. The "yellow stars" has her attention. "Yes, honey, I know. I hope we're not too late. Would it be too much of a favor if . . ." Nana glances at the bike and Marigold steps around and opens a small side entry gate.

"Why Ms. Hawkins, I'm surprised you'd have to ask." She opens the gate, and Josh scoots the bike behind her inside the ticket booth.

"Thanks, sugar. We'll be back after the second race." Nana looks quickly up at the inky sky--already spitting large raindrops. "Now, Josh, what about that hot dog?"

Josh hesitates, rubbing his untied tennis shoe against the metal rail, "Uh, I don't know if . . ."

And if reading his thoughts, Nana pushes back her hat and looks straight into his eyes, "I would trust my soul with Marigold."

Josh feels the color rise in his freckled cheeks, and he leans down to tie the shoe, feeling slightly ashamed. But to his surprise, it is Marigold that steps out of the gate and picks out a shiny parasol, saying-- "You're a lucky boy to have such a bike." She smiles, placing the parasol over the bike basket.

Nana places two dollars down on the gate, "It's a lucky bike to have such a boy." Then, she picks out a parasol, snaps it open and waves good-bye over her shoulder, "Can't doodle. We'll scoot before we're all standing in a mud puddle and using this lucky bike as a boat." She takes off, then whirls, actually does a pirouette, and walks back to Marigold, "Gracious, honey, almost forgot to pay. Here you go then." Nana opens an envelope that looks tattered around the edges and tea-stained (perhaps Kabusha tea stained, Josh grins); then she twirls the parasol, "Toottles, Marigold."

"Good luck, Hawkins. May the Goddess of Greyhounds go with you."

Josh catches up with Nana whom he realizes can be quite fast. "You think it will be safe, Ms. Hawkins?"

"Safe? Nana closes the parasol, and springs open a large umbrella with polka dots, "Never thought about it. Why I never think about things being safe."

"Why'd you buy the parasol if you . . ." Josh doesn't finish his thought.

"The parasols are Marigold's 'tips'. Isn't she just like a duck? All quivery, you can almost see her tail feathers. Got a heart as big as heaven. Now, wonder where hc could be?"

Josh follows in and around race track fans, also hurrying for the main entrance. He suddenly realizes that he's hungry and he thinks about the hot dog. He can taste that hot dog, oozing with catsup; maybe he'll splurge and go for some pickle relish or chili . . .

"Who? Wonder where who is?"

"Big Sam." Nana makes a sharp turn past a hot dog stand and a tray of the most delicious looking, greasy french fries and all but skips up an escalator. Josh, eyeing the fries, follows. He pushes up his cap, turns it sideways, with the dog ears flapping and grins up at the tiny woman, more like a sparrow with flecks of sunlight in her white, white hair.

"Josh, I've always found that what you expect, you'll find. Expect your bike to be stolen, and you'll lose your bike. Expect a lemon pie in your Banyan Tree and you'll find something delicious. It's the kind of magic a small child has when he places a tooth under his pillow and wakes up to a silver dollar!"

The escalator disappears into a second floor crowded with even more fans; but the air is cooler, lighter. Nana skips the last step, lands and smiles back at Josh and links her arm around his, "Don't ever lose the child inside of you, Josh. It's the most precious gift you can give your grown-up self."

"Are we still talking about hot dogs?" Josh takes off his glasses, looking straight into her eyes.

She meets his gaze, knowing that the part of him that needs to hear, does hear. Then, she nods, "That's exactly what I'm talking about-- "Hot dogs." Then, she does something really crazy. She links her arm around his and whispers in a half-talked, half-sung song, "Hot dogs. Armor hot dogs. What kind of kids eat Armor Hot dogs? Fat kids. Skinny kids. Kids who climb on rocks."

Josh, slightly embarrassed, feeling the redness rise to his freckled cheeks, tightens his shoulder blades, hoping to become invisible beneath his t-shirt. And then, he blurts out "Hot Dogs." Because he's catching on that he knows absolutely no one in this hot dog eating, dog track crowd of strangers. He whistles along. They pass the betting windows, round a corner and run right smack into one of the biggest, tallest, probably the most glittery man Josh has ever seen. He speaks, not surprisingly in a deep raspy voice, "Miss Hawkins, where you been girl? You late."

"Hello, Big Sam."

Josh slips back behind Nana as she walks up to Sam's betting window. Sam, a human jewelry store with glittering gold in his ears, nose and lips, holds up a racing form, curiously marked with yellow stars. "I think maybe you stand Sam up, yeah?"

Nana reaches for the form. Her entire demeanor changes. She pulls out a pair of spectacles (with the Wal-Mart tag dangling) and motions Josh to step forward. She is clearly distracted by whatever the stars signal. "Sam, this is my friend, Josh. He lives behind the Banyan Tree--or perhaps it's the other way round. Josh gave a hand with the pies this year."

"Oh yeah?" Sam, obviously impressed, sticks out his hand (also decorated in gold and silver and diamonds) and slaps Josh's small hand. "You's de man. Give me some." Sam slaps Josh's hand, grinning. "You's de man. Hawkins don't let nobody mess with her pies."

"Big Sam's from Haiti. He came over on a small boat. How's your political asylum claim, Sam?"

"Not so good, Ms. Hawkins. I think maybe, maybe they don't believe me when I say bad things happen to Sam when he talk about Papa Doc and Baby Doc."

"But you mustn't give up hope, Big Sam. There's a very fine lawyer with that Committee for International Human Rights; I'll tell him about you. I met him at the market. He bought one of the pies."

Sam beams. He grows taller. Nana shakes her head, mentally making a note of all this and then, quickly switches to the present situation. Going up on tip-toe, she peers over the betting booth and whispers, "How many we got, Sam? These Wal-Mart glasses are too strong."

Sam takes back the racing form, pointing to the stars. "Two, maybe three. But not today."

"What about Whisper?"

Sam winces, "Wagon going take Whisper if he don't break the gate."

"I was afraid of that, honey. Well, thank you." She slips her reading glasses back into the giant bag, turns and then, remembering, smiles-- "Oh, how's Ella?"

A huge greyhound, mostly white with one brown spot, leaps up from behind the window. Her tail slaps gingerly against Big Sam's face. Nana scratches the dog behind his ears, "Oh there you are, Ella. Gracious, I wouldn't have known you. Well, thanks. We better get out to the track. Bye, Sam." Nana reaches into her skirt pocket and hands the dog a small dog biscuit; the dog shivers, drooling.

"Go. You go. Before it's too late."

"Too late for what?" Josh lets Eella lick his hand, which is salty with perspiration from all the clapping on the trolley, then he turns and follows Nana out through swing glass doors leading into the grandstand section. The crowd outside is buzzing; a feverish excitement stings the hot air. Josh hurries to keep up with Nana; they make their way through the dog fans, licking melting ice cream cones, snow cones dripping sugary watermelon, lime or strawberry onto t-shirts already stained with mustard from oozing hot dogs. The crowd waits expectantly, eating, drinking, licking delicious foods with intoxicatingly delicious smells. Josh is suddenly very hungry. He glances around for a hot dog vendor but Nana is quickly disappearing up steps, into a box area in the front section of the seats. She squeezes in behind a gentleman and his granddaughter and stares solemnly down at the track, where about eight greyhounds are parading out onto the hot track. Led by young Hispanic workers, the dogs are elegant, poised and almost magnificent creatures.

Josh glances at the track and then at the little curly red haired child eating a juicy hot dog. She smiles back, wipes her mouth. Giggles. Josh leans against the rail, talking out loud--"Mustard? Ketchup?"

Nana isn't listening. He whistles. "Hot dogs." Then, stops. There's something bigger than hot dogs going on. He's missed something. He stands up, trying to see what it is that Nana sees. Trying to see what is 'invisible except to those who see with the heart.' He squints against the glaring sun and slowly, as he opens his eyes to 'whisper or dream eyes", he feels a pulse-beat, an energy rising up from within. A rhythm in the slow stride of the greyhounds. One dog is out of sync with the others. One dog lags behind, head low, eyes swallowing fear. Which dog? He feels a small hand touch his shoulder; it's the little girl with the hot dog, offering him her binoculars--"Would you like to use them?" She smiles.

Freaky. How could she know. Maybe she's not really a little girl. Maybe she's like this greyhound guardian angel--in disguise.

"Sure." Josh sounds cool. He looks through the binoculars at each dog. Still, he can't see which dog is causing Nana so much pain. He puts down the binoculars, considers asking her but she's entirely focused on the track. The little girl's voice catches him by complete surprise, "I'm pulling for Whisper, Number Five."

"Oh yeah?" Josh puts down the binoculars and stares hard at the greyhounds, entering the starting gate. Nana is very, very still. Josh hesitates, then ventures, "Which one are you on?"

Nana is far away, but she answers him, "On?"

"Betting on? Isn't that why we're here? To win some money for the Christmas angel. Didn't Big Sam give you a hot tip?"

Looking

"No, Josh, it's not like that. If Whisper doesn't break the gate, and finish the race then ..." Her voice disappears into the crackling sound of a loud speaker; the track announcer booms out, "Here goes, Lucky."

There's a loud sizzling noise, like firecrackers spitting on the Fourth of July and Lucky, the mechanical rabbit, breaks out in front of the greyhounds. Suddenly, the greyhounds take off, yelping. As the dogs pound the hot dust, the rabbit whizzes out, flying at an incredibly fast speed. The dogs flash past. There is nothing but speed. High energy. Heart-pounding. Speed. Josh stares through the binoculars, mesmerized, but feeling a sickening wave of fear, "If Whisper doesn't break the gate, then what?"

"Come on, Whisper. Come on girl." Nana's fingers wrap around the metal railing in a clenched fist. She's racing with the greyhounds. With the dog who now holds her heart. Josh's hand grabs the railing; he leans forward, feeling the hot metal--slick and sweaty--repelling his grasp. He's so hot; his t-shirt clings to his skin and he stares. Hard. Trying to be fully present.

Suddenly, the dogs raise their heads, sniffing the air. Elegant. Sleek. Their presence changes the pulse-beat of the crowd. He listens, leaning in closer, closer to the railing. He can hear the soft thud of their paws against the dust and dirt. Hear their breathing, their panting. Then, he sees the light. Unexpectedly. Scorching the slip of purple sky behind a row of palms. And this light is unlike anything he has ever seen. The dogs are suddenly luminous, burning, as if their skin were on fire. But the light is most intense around Number Five; the dog's silhouette flickers, elongates and burns. Suddenly, the announcer's voice booms out and the greyhounds stretch out their sleek bodies and fly.

"Come on, Whisper. Come on, girl." Nana's fingers wrap around Josh's hand stuck to the railing; but her hand is hot, curling tight into a clenched fist. She is no longer present beside Josh. She has gone down there. To the race track. With the greyhounds. With the bandaged Whisper who is barely staying with the pack.

A handsome, strong-muscled greyhound whips past the turn, yelping, and takes the lead. "Lucky" races ahead, taunting, teasing, always just a stride ahead, always just within a nose reach. The dogs fan out, then almost magically, catch up with the lead dog. Elegant gazelles in motion. Slender wisps against the scorching sun, the heavy stillness, they own the track. Theirs is the race. Bewitched are the fans. Until, finally, Lucky takes the last turn, followed by a black and white greyhound who pounds the track, racing, flying, winning. The fans are suddenly one fan-standing, staring. And there is a moment, a breathless moment of sheer suspense, in which all eyes fix upon the lead dog. The track announcer feeds the crowd's fever, calling out hoarsely, "And it's Chillean Holiday with Colorado Rocket coming up on the inside."

Thunder rumbles. A plane's engine rises over the roar of the crowd. Josh glances up, facing the glare of sizzling light breaking through clouds the color of indigo, then deepening into a fierce ominous black. The rain will break any second. Josh feels the first large raindrop; he holds his hands up, cupped, catching the rain to cool his hands, to splash against his burning cheeks. Then, it comes. Rain. Warm rain. Pelting from the sky. Newspapers and racing forms, shoot up as make-shift umbrellas in the ecstatic crowd.

The dogs battle it out to the finish. Josh tugs on Nana's sleeve but she is far away. In a place apart from heavy rain and crowds, in a sacred portal where there is no time, where the human heart hears the prayers of animals. Animals who are wounded. Hurt animals. Lonely animals. Nana's voice, low and resonant, rises up from deep with the very essence of her being and it seems to Josh that he is eavesdropping on an angel, "Whisper, don't give up. Please, please don't give up."

The rain comes. Heavy. Silky. Pouring from the steamy sky, a cloak of grey, vast, dense, hovering over the track. Lightning flashes. "Oos" and "ahs" escape from the lips of those willing to tough it out.

The track announcer's voice calls the race, "On the outside turn, it's Colorado Rocket taking the lead. Stealing up from the inside it's Miss Gypsy Rose--gaining speed. And here comes Lilly rue."

As the rain beats down, the crowd scatters. Josh starts down the steps, heading back towards the Club House. He glances back over his shoulder at Nana, drenched. Her white hair dripping in lose strands, her eyes determined, pinballs of grey steele, staring at the lame, white-faced Whisper who is trailing towards the finish. Walkers, mostly Hispanic young men, hurry out onto the now muddy track and quickly slip leads onto the greyhounds. Whisper tilts her head, gazes at the crowd, as if she felt the one human spirit who was still cheering her on and the greyhound, thin, shivering, becomes almost radiant, luminous in that one split second when she sees Nana, standing alone, clapping, cheering in a hoarse voice--

"You did it, Whisper. You finished the race!" She closes her eyes, and in a softer voice, offers a word of hope to the limping greyhound, a prayer, "Let us now run with perseverance the race set before us. We shall mount up with wings of eagles; we shall run and not be weary, walk and not be weak. We shall soar with the wings of eagles."

Then, an older man, in a mustard rain cape, yanks a metal choker around Whisper's neck and drags the exhausted, frightened greyhound towards the backside of the track, in the exact opposite direction from the kennel. Nana grabs Josh's arm, "Hurry, Josh. Hurry. We haven't much time. We're all she's got now."

Nana, with an enormous surge of strength, pushes Josh down the steps, into the main grandstand section. Josh follows; they walk, then break into a run, following the fenced track around towards the backside. Nana never lets the mustard cape or the poor Whisper out of her sight. Breathless, heart-pounding, Josh follows. The rain soaks through his t-shirt; his skin feels taut against the wetness and yet despite all this, Josh feels an excitement that comes from deep within his being. He follows without questioning where or why or which path might lead beyond the narrow opening in the back fence. As they scrunch beneath a break in the fence, Nana and Josh both step into a pool of yelping, barking dogs.

They slip in and around the cages that lie in the shadow of tall palms and thick pines. The greyhounds stare at Nana through the wire; then the barking melts into a whine, as if they sensed that she was coming into their midst to rescue one of their own kind. Nana whistles for the greyhound "Whisper" through purple lips.

"Whisper, Whisper?" Her mouth puckers into a low whistle that blows softly, then shrill over the rain and the dogs. Josh hears a faint whine. He turns in circles, behind Nana, his eyes searching with her eyes. They almost turn in circles, spinning as children do with their arms held out to their sides and gliding over the warm air; then, they approach each cage. There is a slight whisper; then silence. Eerie. Penetrating. And from the hot ground, steam rises, bathing the backside in a grey fog that covers the cages. Josh's heart beats wildly. What if they don't find Whisper--what then?

Nana faces the grayness; she calls again and again, beating back the rain with her own wild spirit. Somewhere close, in a concrete block wall pen that looks more like a garbage dumpster than a pen for a dog, a sound escapes. Rising above the rain. Not a whimper but a voice of courage. Nana turns, leans down and thrusts her hand into the dank grayness inside the locked cell. A tongue licks her palm, then a black nose appears and finally, Whisper, muzzled and tied to a metal hook in the floor, appears. Josh sees drops of blood on Nana's sleeve; she misses it at first and cradles the dog's head in her lap.

"Nana." Josh points to the bloodstain on the cage floor.

"Oh ..." Nana's voice trembles with anger. "Not even a pail for water. No kibble." She cups her hands, catching the rain and offers it to the greyhound. The dog licks her fingers. It is a gesture of humble gratitude. The dog's eyes gaze straight into Nana's eyes. Josh stands still, aware that he is being allowed to witness something beyond his understanding--something deeply gallant and kind. Nana takes off her drenched hat and holds it up to the rain. She twists the hat, poking it sideways through the bars, allowing the dog to sniff the wet straw, to drink the rain. Gently, she loosens the dog's collar, releases the muzzle and then picks the lock with a pin from her hair. The cage door opens, creaking. Whisper, however, crouches low, frightened, shoulders hunched. Refusing to move. Nana reaches into the cage, cradles the dog in her arms, wrapping her own thin shoulders around the quivering animal.

The rain pounds down, harder and harder. As if it warning of something ominous, of a darkness waiting. Without a voice. Without a face. But real. Josh feels the fear, tenses. Suddenly, the greyhounds yelp; whining in a loud, eerie sound that pierces the stillness, the pounding rain. Nana stops, listens. Josh hears the wheels spinning gravel, grinding against wet sand. He follows Nana's gaze as she stares at a small grey "wagon" with a metal cage, moving up through the pens, heading straight towards the concrete block. The man driving the truck stops outside the pen; he climbs out of the truck. Josh pulls Nana back against the wall, staring at the man's yellow rain slicker as he kneels down and opens the concrete block cage with the metal gate. He whirls around, furious.

Josh steps out into the rain.

For a minute, the man doesn't see Josh. He climbs back into his wagon and moves slowly along the concrete wall, coming straight towards the small narrow path where Nana is hiding with the dog. Suddenly, Josh moves out onto the gravel path, straight towards the wagon. Josh can feel the man's stare; there is a sickeningly sweet smell of cigar and something else--something Josh can't quite name. But the smell is strong, over-powering and repulsive. Just as the wagon reaches Josh, the window rolls down and the man shoots out an arm, grabbing Josh by the shoulder, "Hey kid?"

Josh whirls, facing the man. He stares at the man's arm, tattooed with black snakes. The man spits, narrowly missing Josh's face. "Kid, she's a dog-napper. You go to jail for that."

Josh looks directly into the man's eyes, and sneezes, really loud. He takes off his glasses, which are fogging up and sneezes again. And again. The sneeze sprays out into the man's face. "Oh, sorry. I've got a bad . . . ah-chew . . . cold. I just got back from an exchange program with . . . ah-ah-chew China. But don't worry, it's not SARS or anything." Josh blows his nose and coughs. The man with the snake tattoos immediately rolls up his window. Through steamy glass, he stares at Josh. For a second, Josh isn't sure whether the man believes him; then, he turns the wagon back towards the other side of the track. Josh waits, watching the man and the wagon disappear before he motions to Nana. "Hurry. I'm not sure whether he believed me."

"Well done, Josh. Houdini couldn't have thought of a better trick." She hands him a handkerchief "Blow your nose,."

"I was fakin' it." He starts to hand back the handkerchief, creamy white lace with the initials "MEJ" embroidered in blue thread.

"No, keep it. We better hurry or you and Whisper really will catch cold." Nana slips her sweater around Whisper, "Here." She lowers her head, walking out into the rain, making her way towards the entry gates. The distance between the concrete wall and the sea of asphalt is overwhelmingly great; but Nana goes forward, undaunted, carrying the dog. Josh hurries and as they finally reach the open grandstand section, he sees white light shooting down through clouds, connecting earth and sky. Nana sees the light and smiles, "A portal to heaven."

She slips a ribbon from her waist around Whisper's head and guides the dog towards the entry gates. As they reach the turn-style, Marigold appears from behind a racing form. She brushes her finger across her chapped lips, then places a kiss on the dog's forehead, "Bless ya, Miss Hawkins. I don't know how they do it. Such sweet, gentle beings."

Then she hurries them on, glancing warily at a track official only a few feet away, "Oh and this belongs to you. I kept her dry with the racing forms." As she wheels out the bike, a dozen or more racing forms catch the wind and scatter. Marigold pretends to chase them, waving Nana on and Josh catches on that the flying papers are a distraction--a way for Nana to escape with the greyhound. Josh hurries to catch up, walking the bike through puddles, his head bent down, cap pulled low over his eyes. He wipes his glasses, which keep steaming up. The parking lot is one hot, steam bath. Nana waves at a hot dog vendor, "Oh Chickee, we need two, no three hot dogs."

Nana takes out the paper envelope; and coins, mostly pennies and nickels, spill out from the soaked paper, disappearing beneath the stand. Chickee, a splash of lavender flowers beneath a great straw hat, purrs to a tiny bird sitting on her shoulder, "On the house, Miss Hawkins, and I do hope they're not too soggy."

Nana clucks to the bird, a sparrow, shaking her head, "It's too bad you're not selling umbrellas, Chickee. Well now, Merry Christmas. Charlotte or . . . oh dear, is it Emma?"

The tiny sparrow cocks her head and looks straight at Josh. The bird's eyes don't blink. And the staring is a rather curious thing for a wild bird to do. But then, Josh realizes that he has never seen a sparrow sitting on a woman's shoulder. Nana breaks his fascination with a whistle, "Merry Christmas, Chickee."

112

Chickee laughs, a bird-sort of laugh with lots of feathers and breathy "oos" and she hands a hot dog to Josh who takes it, fixes his glasses (steaming up again) and tries hard to stare at something other than the bird. Nana breaks her hot dog into small pieces and feeds them to the shivering greyhound who is starved. Then, she says simply, "Josh, Whisper didn't have a chance in that cage."

Josh glances up at her, surprised by her sudden change in mood. "I, I know."

She smiles, a tired smile. "No, of course not. But not everyone sees with their heart. I don't think so much about what's right or wrong. I spent a life-time living that way. Always judging others and always judging myself. Now, I just try and do what I believe will bring the greatest good to the most people, or animals. Old dogs don't deserve to be muzzled, to be starved . . . and certainly, they don't deserve to be killed."

"Miss Hawkins, you don't have to explain anything."

"Thank you, Josh. Now, lets get you to that trolley." She starts back across the parking lot, which is quite steamy and all puddles. The trolley is just pulling around the corner; Dominic is clanging the bell and Josh feels a great sense of adventure as he walks beside Nana, still cradling the greyhound. Then, Chickee whistles. Loud. Strong. Nana turns and sees the funny bird woman waving and whistling.

"Oh dear, what on earth could have happened?" Nana hesitates, debating whether to go back to help Chickee or trudge forward and get Josh and Whisper safely on the trolley. She sighs, turning around, "I'll have to go back." The dog starts to whine. He pushes his nose up out of Nana's wrap, gazing into Nana's eyes, licking her face. "What is it girl?"

Josh sees the man with the tattoos walking with two police officers--heading straight towards the trolley. He turns around; Nana also sees the officers and they circle back to Chickee's stand, "Go on, Josh. They won't be looking for you." They realize that they are in full view of the tattoo man who is constantly looking back around. Then a "Yew-hew" catches them by surprise. The voice, trilled and soft, sounding bird-like, comes from only a few feet away. Josh turns to see Chickee waving at them from behind a huge umbrella. She has the bird on her shoulder now and sweeps in front of them, shielding Nana from sight of the tattoo man. The bird suddenly takes off and lands smack on Nana's head-- "Oh dear, Chickee, what is it?"

"Come here, Emma. Thinks your hair is a nice soft nest, she does. Oh dear, not a minute to lose. That awful man with the tattoos came out of nowhere, trailing you and that poor dog, I reckon. He's got two policemen with him and I over-heard them say they were looking for a lady with a greyhound, heading straight for the trolley, they are."

"Gracious." Nana slowly raises her hands and gently lifts the bird out of her hair. "Go home, dear." The bird flies back to Chickee; sits there and cocks her head. "Bless you, honey. Why Whisper and I would have been walking straight into that terrible wagon. Bless you."

"You better step round to my booth till they decide you ain't on the trolley and come back lookin' for you. There's not enough room to whip a cat in, but you'll be safe and then we'll se about how to get ya home."

Nana ducks behind Chickee's umbrella, "Oh thank you, Chickee." They practically stumble smack into a grocery cart sitting smack in the blistering sun in the middle of the parking lot. Nana arches her back, leans down and drops Whisper into the basket. She quickly covers the dog with her sweater. "There now."

Josh starts to push the cart. Nana places her small, freckled hands over his, "Josh, they're not looking for a small boy with a heart as big as heaven. Go on now. Get on the trolley."

"Oh, but I can't leave you. Not now. Besides, I don't understand. Why are they looking for Whisper? Why can't they just let things be?"

Chickee trills, "Oh it isn't about the dog. It's about the money. Insurance. It has nothing in the world to do with Whisper."

"Josh, Chickee's right. We'll talk later. Right now, the best thing you can do to help Whisper is to get on that trolley. Now go no."

The trolley bell clangs loudly; there's a sense of urgency, perhaps warning in the bell and Josh can't help but wonder if Dominic is trying to warn them. "But I can't just leave you, with that hurt ankle and . . ."

"Yes, you can. I'll be just fine. Why, I've gotten out of tougher scrapes than this." She looks at Chickee and winks, "Remember that dog that wouldn't stop yelping. Why everybody at the track kept looking at him and I finally had to let him down and pretend I was walking him around for Adoption. Of course, no one wanted to adopt a greyhound who thought it was a beagle."

Josh hesitates, glancing towards the clanging trolley. Nana seems to read his thoughts, "Go one. Perhaps you and Dominic can figure out how to out-fox that tattooed snake-handler."

Josh blushes; the freckles along his cheeks and nose deepen and his glasses steam-up. He swallows hard, hands the remaining piece of hot dog to Nana and in a very grown-up voice says, "Good-bye Miss Hawkins." It's all he can possibly say without tearing up, right there in that melting tar, hotter than blazes parking lot. Then, he turns towards the trolley, heading straight towards the cigar-smoking man with the snake tattoos crawling up the skin of his back and arms. Josh takes off, waving, calling out--

"I won. I won."

Dominic slows the trolley, clangs the bell and turns the trolley in a tight circle. He opens the door. Josh squeezes between the two police officers and the tattoo-man and jumps up onto the trolley, murmuring a quick, "Sorry. Excuse me." The man with the tattoos spits out his cigar and tries to grab Josh who scoots in behind Dominic. Sensing trouble, Dominic turns on the charm, stands, and towering over the officers, grins, "Is hot, yes? Is very, very hot?

The police officer glances up at Dominic, "Look, we're sorry about the delay. We had a tip to try the trolley."

"Try the trolley? Well, come on." Dominic shakes with laughter, covering for Josh who scoots down behind the driver's seat.

The second officer isn't quite as polite, "This guy here says you know a lady, sometimes rides the trolley. She may be the one stealing the greyhounds."

Dominic smiles, steps back, "Please, take a look."

The officers and tattoo man step up onto the few entry steps, then walk towards the back of the trolley, looking down every aisle.

Finally, they stop in front of Josh who sits still, holding onto his bike, pretending he's asleep. Dominic clangs the bell, calling out "Old Naples."

The officers turn and step down out of the trolley, motioning for the tattoo man to follow. He glares at Josh but has no choice but to leave. One of the officers glances back up at Dominic, "Well, if you see anyone fits that description--"

"Of course." Dominic gives the bell one last clang, signaling that it's all right for Josh to open his eyes. Josh catches a fleeting glimpse of the tattoo man walking off with the officers. As the door closes, Josh takes off his glasses and stares at his tennis shoes. The bell rings out, clanging steadily over the rain. Josh glances up in the mirror and sees Dominic watching him, "Ms. Hawkins--she is crazy lady."

Josh scuffs his tennis shoe against the metal floorboard, "I--I don't really know her very ..."

"Imagine-- giving her own pair of shoes to a little child didn't have none ... or feeding migrant workers out of her own kitchen window or savin' old dogs from the Wagon. Got eyes for seeing the invisible ones. She's crazy, but ain't we the lucky ones to know her?"

Dominic guides the trolley back towards the main highway. Josh watches the Bonita Springs Dog Track disappear beneath a double rainbow--a sign, perhaps. Then, Christmas music sprinkles out over the rain. Dominic's radio, Josh smiles. He presses his face close to the window, aware that the trolley has stopped and that the Second Avenue Baptist Church Choir is now crowding onto the trolley. Drenched, but in high spirits, they spread out over the trolley like melted maple sugar, fanning the No-See 'ems and squeezing the rain from their shoes.

Josh scoots over, making room for a woman in flip flops with a pink rose (smelling like honeysuckle) to sit down beside him. Suddenly, the radio disc jockey, Pippa, breaks in over the "Dance of the Sugar Plum Fairy.-- "Somewhere out there a Mrs. Santa Claus is waiting. She might be the sweet little lady right next door or the lady at the McDonald's drive-through or your Great Aunt Myrtle. What makes someone you know the perfect Mrs. Santa Claus? I'm

Pippa for 'Lovin', Lookin' or Leavin'" helping to find Kris Kringle the love of his life."

A flip-flop suddenly goes up, and dusty toes wiggle. The honeysuckle lady giggles, sighs and pops open a can of root beer, "Santa Claus looking for a wife. Now that's cute. That's just real cute." She sips the root beer, closes her eyes and hums. Josh stares out the window and sees Nana, walking slowly towards a dumpster. She sifts through several plastic bags, takes out a colorful scarf. Josh glances up at Dominic, smiles. They both gaze out the window at Nana, pushing the dog in the grocery cart. Whisper is wearing her purple scarf and Nana is ... she's actually roller blading.

CHAPTER SEVENEEN

The Royal Poinsettia Country Club is lit-up with a zillion stars, burning brilliantly from palm trees, roof tops and a gigantic fake chimney. Josh, leaning over the rail of the trolley, stares at the display of glistening white lights and lets out a soft, "Wow" which almost awakens his seat-mate, the lady in the flower flip-flops. He pops his last piece of chewing gum into his mouth and stares through his reflection at the party tent, a giant white balloon on the silvery landscape. A white breath of snow falls from a fake snow-blower. Josh pushes open the window and holds out his hand, catching a few of the snowflakes.

"Wow!"

He leans his head out the window, sticks out his tongue and stares up into the spiraling whiteness and for a flickering breath of time, he sees four hooves, flying. Kicking snowflakes. Pounding the soft breeze. Four hooves. Yes. Unmistakable. And then, four legs. Swift and . . . yes, a tail. And, Josh blinks. He feels a strong hand on the back of his neck; then a yank, "Get in here. Close that window. Right now."

Josh sinks back into the seat, staring at the gardenia pinned onto the woman's dress which is flip-flopping, up and down. "Sorry." Josh manages to sneak a quick look back up at the sky. Nothing. No hooves. No tail. No reindeer. And yet . . . he has seen something. The trolley turns onto Harbor Drive. The magic of glistening lights disappears behind the yellow glow of street lights. Disappointed, Josh pulls his knees up close to his chest. He feels a sudden loneliness, a missing. A missing for his friend. For the adventure and freedom of her life. He slips his fingers into the hole in his jeans--making the hole bigger. He digs into his pockets, hoping for a bit of chocolate and feels the handkerchief. Slowly, as if it were magical, he brings the handkerchief out into the dim light. He traces the initials with his fingers, wondering if the handkerchief actually belongs to his friend, Nana Hawkins. Then, a warm surge of feeling wells up inside of him. It is an intensity-a strong feeling of belonging. Of being one with the trolley and the lady in the flip-flops. Of being connected with Dominic and . . .

The reindeer is flying just outside the trolley window. Josh feels its presence before actually hearing the harness bell. When he turns, he knows that the reindeer is near. Very, very near. He looks at Blitzen. Blitzen looks at him. And the reindeer winks. Then, sleigh and reindeer disappear up into the billows of fake snow being blown out onto the parking lot of the Royal Poinsettia Country Club.

Josh blows the biggest bubble he has ever blown in his entire life--"Oh my . . . " But he doesn't finish because the lady in the flip-flops reaches over and zings the bubble with her red painted finger-nail. Pop. "Spit that out, honey. It'll git in your hair and on your eyelashes. I knew a kid went to sleep with chewing gum and . . ."

But Josh is flying with the reindeer.

CHAPTER EIGHTEEN

Cape dips a paper cup out into the sprinkling whiteness, then he wiggles his nose and tops the frozen snow with the most delicious cherry flavoring, then a sprinkle of watermelon, a dash of cotton candy and a daring sip. Wonderful. He props up his feet and enjoys the "instant snow cone", while taking in the stars.

"Blitz, keep an eye out for that country club, Royal Poinsettia. Should be lots of those red flowers." Cape closes his eyes then opens then when the sleigh takes a sudden dip. He is face to face with a small boy--staring straight at Blitz, sleigh and elf from a curious-looking motor wagon. Cape instantly picks up the reigns and guides Blitz back up through the falling snow.

"Blitz, what was that all about?"

Blitz of course retorts that "that's the boy" but Cape is much too distracted by the powerful snow blower which is blowing his tux jacket open, about to take his top hat and somersaulting the sleigh upside-down into a near nose-dive. It's actually Blitz who gets them out of the grip of the snow-blower but of course Cape would probably see it in a much different light.

The sleigh lands quietly, if not quite gently, in the middle of a parking lot, complete with golf carts and a couple of limousines. Cape squeezes into a cummerbund and jumps out of the sleigh. He offers the rest of the snow cone to Blitz, "All right. Just take a little R&R. I'll check out Sugar. How will I know her?" He takes out the piece of paper and reads, "Red." She'll be wearing red. Okay. Will, wish me luck."

Cape takes off, merrily whistling and enters what has to be the most dazzling party tent ever seen by an elf. As he ducks through a flap, Cape steps into a Winter Wonderland. Terribly ritzy with a frozen stream (complete with ice skaters), twinkling white lights on palms and pines, white-clothed tables with small glass tanks filled with goldfish. Cape lets out a low whistle which gets the attention of a perky young elf. She smiles, offers him a party favor of an exotic drink and curtseys,

"Welcome to the Royal Poinsettia Country Club's Christmas Gala. Do you have your invitation?"

Cape looks closely at the young elf, "Are you … do I know you?"

She blushes, "I don't think so."

He goes up on his toes and checks out her ears which are small and sweet. Disappointed, he sighs, "No, guess not. For a second there I thought maybe Jingles had sent in a back-up, you know, to help with the situation."

Her blue doe-like eyes widen, "Is there a 'situation' sir?"

"No, nothing to worry about. Oh, I'm meeting a Ms. Sugar St. Clair? Have you seen her?"

The pretty elf is relieved. "So, you're meeting someone. Does she have your invitation?"

Cape pulls out the envelope from Sugar and takes out the invitation. "This it?"

"Thank you, sir. Ms St. Clair's table is by the dance-floor." She points across the room at a table near the band. Cape nods, and disappears into the crowd of sequins, feathers and furs. About a foot from the St. Clair table, Cape stops. A very attractive woman in red is staring into a gold compact. She rubs her tongue across her teeth, then freshens her breath with a minty spray and applies lipstick with a tiny brush. It is her lips which amaze Cape for they are quite full, pouty lips that seem a little too large for the woman's face. Suddenly, Sugar catches Cape's reflection in her mirror and shuts the compact, breaking a nail.

"Oh Sugar!"

"So, you're Sugar." Cape moves around in front of Sugar, and bows. "Caperton Elf."

Sucking on the broken nail, Sugar holds out a limp red-gloved hand, "Pleasure, Mr. Elf."

"Excuse me, is anyone sitting here?"

"Oh no."

Cape starts to pull out the chair, then changes his mind. "Ms. St. Clair, we got your letter. Would you, would you like to dance?"

Sugar comes to life at the invitation. She grabs Cape's hand and whirls him out onto the dance-floor. "I was born to boogey."

Cape reconsiders the invitation. "Perhaps, we should talk first."

"Fire away." Sugar shimmies; she even blows fish-kisses with her lips while dancing gracefully, circling Cape who is blushing. Sugar dances in close to Cape and looks down at the top of his head. He looks up at her. And there is this intense moment--almost as if each realized that the other was not who they originally hoped for. Sugar breaks the awkward, stunned silence.

"Aren't you a little ..."?

"Short?"

"Well, now that you mention it."

(Sugar does an elegant rendition of the cha-cha. Cape tries to follow.)

"Actually, I'm a little tall for an elf."

Sugar stops can canning. She looks at Cape. Really looks at him and takes off his hat. She stares at his ears, which are twitching. Cape catches on and shoots up his hands to hold down his ears. But it's no use. The ears are tingling, turning pink. He gasps. Sugar starts to laugh; she bends over with laugher. Squeals come out of her lips.

"What is it? Please, ah-ah ..."

She bursts into great hee-haws. Her laughter is very appealing, starting in her throat, sounding like a mockingbird, trilling the air.

"Oh my, your ... look at your ears." She touches the tips of Cape's ears. "They're so cute. And sensuous. They twitch." Sugar giggles, does a low dip. Cape catches her, but it's close.

"Please, we got your letter."

All giggles, Sugar parades around the dance-floor; on-lookers smile, admiring her style. She puckers her lips, "My letter?"

Cape is all business. "'Lovin', Lookin' or Leavin'?"

"Oh THAT LETTER." Sugar twirls in close, does a shimmy, shake, twirls and bats her double-fake eyelashes.

Cape nods, fishing in his pocket for the letter. She stops, stares directly at Cape-- "You're really an elf.

Cape wiggles his ears.

"Is he here? You know who?" Sugar comes to life; she looks around the party tent--searching for Santa.

"No, actually, I'm alone."

She deflates, but keeps dancing. "Oh, I see. You're the scout. The lead elf, so to speak. Checking us out. Well, fire away. Ask me anything. I graduated Magnum Cum Lately before my crown." She winks, not an easy trick with all those eyelashes.

The music picks up speed; the lead singer, a handsome, swarthy young man, Rip the Rock, croons out an Elvis melody. Cape and Sugar dance; she's sensational on her feet (big) Cape holds his own and manages to find the paper while twirling her around-"You believe in Santa Claus?"

"Of course, doesn't everyone?"

"No, Ms. Saint Clair, sadly, only a few grown-ups still believe."

"Oh, so that's a point in my favor." She picks up her gown and does a few kicks, can-can style, turning. Cape tries to follow. Occasionally, their kicks collide and she finally just picks him up and dances with him with his feet slightly off the ground. "Oh, I'm loving this."

"Well, Ms. Saint Clair, your letter . . ." (he opens the pink envelope, takes out the letter, which smells of flowers) "Lavender?"

"No, gardenias. The flowers of love."

"Your letter says that" (reading) ". . . you love children,"

"Doesn't everyone? Oh, look, they're doing the limbo." Sugar drags a reluctant Cape across the dance-floor towards two Christmas Elves holding a limbo stick beneath some dangling mistletoe. Sugar shimmies under the limbo pole. "Oh, and I'm on the Board for Save the Children."

Cape jots down a few notes, walks under the limbo pole without even bending his ears and shoots another question at Sugar-

"And you cook? Says here, you like to cook 'Lobster bisque, salmon almondine, spinach avec la frommage' . . . Santa, Ms. Saint Clair . . ."

"Call me Sugar, elf."

"Well, Sugar-elf, Santa is more of a cookie and cocoa sort of . . ."

"Oh, there he is!" Sugar shoots up, knocks the pole, rings the mistletoe with her heavily sprayed hair and stares past the startled elves at a swarthy, graying man in a red tux.

"Santa?" Cape follows her gaze across the dance-floor.

"I thought you said he wasn't coming. No, Mr. Lloyd Worthington." She whisks out her compact and freshens her lipstick.

A brilliant red. Then, she straightens the mistletoe and hands the limbo stick to the elves. "All right girls, take her down." She dances under the pole--but barely. Cape, on the other hand, walks in and around the pole, barely arching his neck.

"Relax, Sugar-elf. You look absolutely radiant."

"Any lipstick on my teeth?" She smiles, tight-lipped.

"Nope, white as a whistle."

"Okay, so--now where were we, Elverton."

"It's Caperton, not . . ."

"Whatever." She remains calm, bending her back almost to the floor. Her high heel shoes suddenly go air-borne and she dances barefoot. Cape walks easily underneath the pole. He winks at the two Christmas elves--

"Short is beautiful."

"I wonder who he's with. Wonder if William could possibly get him on the show?"

"Who?" Cape is completely lost. Sugar murmurs to herself, bending lower and lower. Cape does a chin-up on the limbo pole, then whirls himself up and over the pole--breaking into an acrobatic routine. The elves let go of the stick and it remains elevated as Cape does several flips, backwards, forward. Then, he catches the stick, does a few tricks with the pole in his teeth, and bows. The Christmas elves applaud, mesmerized. Then, as he does a little spin and remains about a foot off the floor, the elves suddenly drop the pole and disappear into the crowd. As does Mr. Lloyd Worthington-

-in the arms of a cute young thing with red hair and a hot pink gown.

Sugar deflates, sinking down into a chair, "You're very agile, Mr. Elf." She sips a glass of ice water, clicking her painted nails against the glass. Then, she starts on the ice--chewing it, breaking it with her rather big teeth, swallowing ice cubes whole. Cape pulls out a chair and sits down next to Sugar.

"Ms. Saint Clair . . . Sugar, may I ask you something?"

"Fire away." She offers Cape an ice cube; he declines.

"Do you really want to be Mrs. Santa Claus?"

"Of course." She crushes the ice. "Well, not really. William thought it would help the ratings. But I'm allergic to reindeer. Furry things make me sneeze. And I hate the cold. He lives up north, somewhere, doesn't he? Second Star to the Right and straight on till morning?"

"That's Peter Pan. Tell me something, what do you want for Christmas?"

"I want to get my teeth whitened. You know, pearly white caps. I'm tired of sleeping in trays with all this oozing sugary white stuff and I tried the strips--but I kept swallowing them."

Cape pulls his chair in closer; he leans in to Sugar, "What do you really, really want?"

She faces him, spits the ice in the glass, "After my teeth--well, don't tell anybody, but a liposuction on my feet. Me and Cinderella's step-sister have the same shoe size."

She sticks out her leg, exposing her feet. She wiggles her toes. But Cape isn't interested in her feet. He is very serious. "What would it feel like to have small feet?"

"Wonderful. Freeing. Sensational. I could go to the beach, walk barefoot in the sand and not worry about leaving footprints as big as Beowulf. I could be a ballerina. A star!" Her green eyes become luminous; catching all the twinkling lights from the dance-floor. She laughs, "Elf, I've really always wanted to be a movie star and dance like Ginger Rogers."

"Yes. Yes, exactly. I can see you as the new Ginger with great legs, great feet."

"But lets' face it, I'm an aging Miss America with a second rate talk show with big feet."

"You believe in Santa Claus? In Christmas? Do you believe?"

"I said I did."

"Well, say it inside where real Sugar can hear it. And feel great. Feel great about being Ginger Rogers The Second, dancing across the silver screen. Zing it, Sugar. Say it--"I believe in Santa Claus. Close your eyes and feel the energy. Release a deep breath up through your whole body straight out the top of your head. Breathe in, now release with an 'ah-ah'. And sing it--"

Sugar closes her eyes. An eyelash sticks to her cheek; Cape brushes it gently away. She smiles, "I believe in Santa Claus. I believe in . . . "

"Deep breaths. See it. Feel it. Say -ah!"

Sugar whispers over and over "I believe" and starts to cry. Tears stream down, making a sort of streak through the glittery make-up. Cape presses his white handkerchief into her hand. Then, he takes out the emerald bag with the Sugar and Spice and sprinkles some Christmas Magic onto her hair. He does a little pirouette, spins and comes down just in time to see Lloyd Worthington (sans the cute young thing) coming across the floor. Lloyd hesitates; Cape whispers "go on" and steps back. Lloyd doesn't see Cape (for elves are rarely seen by those under a love potion). Lloyd puts his hand on Sugar's bare shoulder. Her eyes shoot open--in shock.

"May I have this dance?"

Sugar's lips part; a sound rises. But she can't speak. She bats her lashes.

"Lloyd Worthington. We met at the Miss America Pageant several years ago . . . " He clears his throat, hoping for a rescue but Sugar only smiles. " . . . I enjoyed your Irish Step Dancing."

"Oh." She giggles. Her voice returns. "The Lloyd Worthington. As in Paramount Producer Worthington."

"I'm no longer with the studio."

"Oh?" She has a fingernail to her lips.

"I have my own production company and I've got a script with your name on it."

"I'm all over it, baby." She blushes; Sugar can't believe she said that in such a hoarse, deep voice.

"It's about a former Miss America who loves to dance."

"Oh no, really! Do tell, Lloyd."

"Would you like to dance? I could tell you about it over a couple of wild moves."

Sugar is caramelizing. She floats out onto the dance-floor in the arms of Lloyd Worthington. She catches a glimpse of Cape, grinning. She waves the handkerchief and Cape mouths, "It's a gift." Sugar starts to dance and whispers "I believe in Santa Claus." But the band stops playing just as she gets the words out of her sweet lips.

Lloyd rescues her, "Ms. Saint Clair, so do I. I always have." He winks. Sugar purrs and Cape helps himself to a couple of apples from a table decoration. Caught by an elf, he gives her a nudge, "For the reindeer."

Then, he skips out of the party tent, whistling along with Rip Rock belting out "White Christmas." He rambles along, past Mercedes and Jaguars--a young man calls out-- "May I help you find your car, sir?"

Cape nods, "Yes, it's a sleigh drawn by a reindeer. I think I left it . . . yes, there it is. Thanks though."

Cape heads towards Blitz, leaving behind a bewildered young parking attendant. Blitz snorts, eyeing the apple. Cape scratches behind the reindeer's ears and holds out the apple. "Well, sorry, Blitz. Sugar's not the one." Blitz sniffs at the emerald bag. "Oh, you're such a detective. Really Blitz, you ought to work for the CIA. I just used a little--just a pinch. For a good cause."

Cape settles into the sleigh; he cracks a handful of pistachios, stretches out his legs and gazes up through the snow at a crescent moon. He takes out the cell phone, starts to ring Jingles, then changes his mind. "Blitz, did I miss something?"

Blitzen snorts, "Yep."

"It was that Flamingo Cottage--right? Had a peaceful energy to it. Lets' take a second look."

Blitzen grins, delighted and snorts-- "Now you're sizzling." And the sleigh rises magically up, up and up until it is just a slip of a shadow cast against the moon.

CHAPTER NINETEEN

For elves and flying reindeer, Time is not. Or rather it is--but rather fluid. So that what might seem but a second in a sleigh, somersaulting about the moon, playing tricks on stars and nose-diving over white-capped waves-- may actually be an entire day or night in "real time". So it is that while Cape enjoys the midnight romp, cracking his pistachios and dozing off to dream of pleasant things (like delicious snow cones and chocolaty chocolate chip cookies), twilight slips into dawn and then, into early morning. And while Cape is flying above the Pier, watching the early fishermen cast their lines, calling to the dolphins and wishing shell-seekers "good luck", quite another adventure is taking place at the Cottage across the street from the Banyan Tree.

Number 5 Peppermint Palm Avenue is a complete and utter disaster!

Nana Hawkins, still on roller blades, spots the fire engine parked outside of the crooked cottage and instantly makes her way up the steps, and flings open the screen door. She stops, staring at the array of rescue workers--two firemen, a paramedic, two other very official looking fellows who are hovering over a stricken Mrs. Upslovsky. They carefully load the babysitter onto a stretcher and as they carry her through the door, Mrs. Upslovsky shoots up and grabs Nana's arm-- "Where's my money? I want my money". This, of course, is said in Russian through clenched teeth. And the grasp on poor Nana's arm is enough to flip an alligator over on his stomach. But Nana, who speaks Russian, is right smack up in Uplovsky's face--

"You're lucky I'm not reporting you to the authorities for child neglect. Why you're . . . " She sniffs Upslovsky's hair, breath and layers of black sweaters-- ". . . drunk."

With this, Mrs. Upslovsky lets out a groan that convinces the paramedics to hurry her out the door. She disappears behind the mesh screen door, but not before several loud hiccups burst out of her tiny mouth which is peeling red lipstick. Nana shuts the door and turns around to see Chad sliding down the banister-

"Well at least she didn't ask you about the babies." He holds out his hand, "Hello, I'm Chad. Your Josh's friend. I'm his brother."

"Of course, Chad. You're the basketball star."

He rubs his fingers through his hair which has changed color and now glows with orange and lime green streaks--"No, I'm the family loser."

Nana doesn't respond right away. Instead, she opens her purse and takes out a small coin. She hands it to Chad, "This belonged to my father. When he left England as a small boy, his father gave it to him. To bring him luck in the new world. He carried it all the way across the ocean; and once, the ship had to stop and everyone had to be very, very still--so that the whales wouldn't capsize the boat." Chad sits down on the bottom step and listens; he doesn't bounce a basketball or drum the rail with his fingers. He is still. Nana continues-- "He carried this coin through Staten Island and on to Iowa where he grew up and started a mill and was very successful. I want you to have it."

"Oh no, I . . ."

"What? You don't think you deserve it? Chad, you deserve great success. You deserve the best that life has to give. There's something in this life that you and only you can do--don't give up on yourself. Believe in that greatness. It's inside of you."

She places the small coin into his hand. He looks at it--turns it over, "What is this?"

"It was a tuppence. My father had an angel imprinted on the coin. Now, do you know where that brother of yours is? I promised him a hot dog."

Chad slips the coin into his pocket; he stands, towering above Nana and arches his arms over his head in a stretch; curiously, he becomes taller, stronger in Nana's presence. "Hey, Josh!" He turns, skips up the stairs, calling out-- "Josh!"

The screen door opens; Josh appears. Chad turns around-- "Where have you been?"

Josh stares at the chair, oozing honey thick with swarming flies; there's a flyswatter resting on the arm and one of Mrs. Upslovsky's slippers. Candy wrappers litter a path from the chair to the television. "Where's Mrs. Upslovsky?"

"I think she might have had a stroke or something. She just passed out. Cold. I called 911 and the paramedics took her off ... "

Josh steps around the chair, looking directly at Nana, "What are you doing here?"

"You forgot your hot dog."

He shakes his head, "You knew something had happened. Do you, do you like spy on us from the Banyan Tree?"

Chad steps between Josh and Nana, "What are you saying man? She came to help."

"It's all right, Chad. No, Josh. I don't spy on you anymore than a child spies on the stars. I simply see what I see. Now, why don't we tidy up this place before your parents arrive home and then lets' head over to Flamingo Cottage for some lunch."

Chad picks up a broom and hands Josh a mop. Josh leans down and picks up a soggy slipper--"I think it's been sterilized with alcohol." He tosses it out the window. Then, he turns to Nana, "Ms. Hawkins, I'm sorry if I sounded ... I don't know. It's just that so much has happened. And I guess I got worried about you and Whisper. Where is Whisper?"

"Mop to floor. Hands to work. Hearts to ... whoops." She slides across the floor, a wet, sticky messs. Josh catches her. "Oh dear, Mrs. Upslovsky was worse than Emma."

"The hurricane, Chad. Not the bird." Josh grins.

"What bird?" Chad checks the birdcage and whistles at Lemon.

"Oh, I'll tell you about it sometime." Josh tosses the mop to Chad who breaks into a wild rendition of a Neil Diamond song,

"Kentucky Woman". Josh starts picking up all the candy wrappers while Nana starts cleaning--with a wonderful whisk broom she discovers behind a closet. In the midst of all this crazy cleaning, Chelsea Rose appears with Baby Ghost (invisible to all except Chelsea and--)

"Oh hello Baby Ghost!" Nana looks up from sweeping.

"Oh --wow. You can see him?"

"Of course. Can't everyone?"

"No. Are you the Lady who lives in the Banyan Tree?"

"I am. And you are Princess Aurora?"

Chelsea giggles, curtseys. And smiles up at Baby Ghost.

"Well, princess, we have some catching up to do on gossip at the Castle, don't we?"

Chelsea takes Nana's hand. They set to work cleaning up after Mrs. Upslovsky. Which is rather like straightening up after a hurricane, a sleepover or Christmas morning. Bing croons over the radio and then, Pippa's voice breaks in--

"Hello all you snowbirds in sunny Southwest Florida. It's almost Christmas and still, no match for St. Nick. Looks like our favorite jolly old elf will be flying solo again this year unless . . . give us a call. Tell us about your pick for Santa's "Mrs.". For 'Lovin', Lookin' or Leavin', I'm Pippa. And here's a love song for all the elves on your Christmas list."

The music disappears into the whirr of a vacuum cleaner and the slushing sound of a mop hitting puddles of spilt "medicine" . And sometime later, the house at Number 5 Peppermint Palm, glistens like a shiny coin, imprinted with the face of an angel.

CHAPTER TWENTY

Inside Flamingo Cottage, the greyhounds sit quietly beneath the table, hoping for a few dropped morsels of pie. But the plates of Chelsea, Chad and Josh are quite licked clean. And the children lean on elbows, eyes wide, listening to Nana' story --

"And there we were. Thunder booming. Lightning cracking across a dusty sky. And Whisper, here, lame as a duck."

Whisper rises, puts his paws on Nana's lap and licks her face.

A breeze from the open window plays tricks on a small white candle on the table. The yellow flame grows tall, flickering lightly. Candles of all shapes and sizes, mostly white but some purple, decorate the cottage windows, the kitchen counter and the small table. They add a touch of celebration to the simple cottage and a' bit of magic to Nana's tale.

Then, from outside, there's the sound of spinning gravel. The dogs raise their heads; a couple of the greyhounds whine and look at Nana. Suddenly, there's a loud knock and a man's voice disturbs the soft stillness of only moments before--

"Ms. Easley, I know you're in there. It's all right. We're not going to hurt you. I'm Officer McClain with the Collier County Police. We just want to see if there might be some kids with you."

Josh glances at Nana, expecting her to be calm. To rise above the fear he feels in his own mind. Chelsea glares at the door and whispers, "Go away, Mr. Dragon."

Chad leans down to the dogs, trying to calm their panic. Josh stands and waits for directions from Nana. But she doesn't move. In a voice surprisingly calm, he says, "Should I . . ."

Nana takes a deep breath, then quietly she leans over and blows out the candle on the table. In turn, she blows out each candle, speaking in a low voice, not looking directly at the children, "Of course, Josh. I always knew it was just a matter of time until this day would come. Had to come. I just didn't know it would come so soon but we have no choice, children, but to open the door." She blows out the last candle, nods to Josh and he steps forward just as a police officer turns the knob and forces open the screen door. He looks at the three children, relieved--"Kids, thank god you're safe. You're all right. Everything's going to be all right."

Dee and Warfield hover behind the Officer, waiting for a signal. The Officer turns, nods and a frantic Dee rushes in and wraps her arms around Chelsea. "Oh my . . ." She holds Chelsea in her arms.

"Mom, you're hurting me."

"Thank heavens, you're all right. Josh! Chad!" She holds Chelsea and turns to the other boys.

Josh steps back, towards Nana, "Mom, it's cool. What's this all about?"

Warfield, miraculously without either cell phone, walks in and starts to take charge, "What happened to Mrs. Kiev?"

Dee wipes her eyes, "Upslovsky, Warfield."

Josh looks at his dad, trying to make sense of why they might be there, "She had something like a stroke. What are you guys doing here?"

"She got drunk and passed out." Chad has his hands on the shivering Whisper, trying to keep the dog calm.

Warfield and Dee both look at each other, "Oh. Oh. Oh."

Warfield pounces on Dee, "Dee, where do you find those people?"

"It was a reputable agency."

Josh intervenes, "Mrs. Hawkins, Dad, Mom, this is Nana Hawkins--she lives here, behind the Banyan Tree and she knows a' lot about our family. She called 911 and probably saved Mrs. Upslovsky's life and us."

There is a chilled silence. The police officer, Warfield and Dee, turn and stare at Nana Hawkins, quietly sipping a cup of Kabusha Tea. She says absolutely nothing. Warfield, uncomfortable with any silence, takes hold of Chad's arm and shoves him towards the door-

"All right. Lets' get home. Now."

Chad shakes his arm free, "What are you doing?"

Josh looks at his mother, "Mom. Dad, wait a minute. Mrs. Hawkins is the one who took care of us."

Dee holds Chelsea in front of her and tries to move Josh towards the door. Her voice is soft, kind--"Why didn't you call us, Josh?"

"I thought you needed time to find a house."

Warfield opens the door, "Lets' go. Chad, is that your basketball?" Warfield swings a reluctant and very confused Chelsea up onto his shoulders and ducks under the tiny door-frame. "Josh, son--we're going home. NOW!"

Josh doesn't budge. He glances at Nana, quietly sipping the tea and then at his mom who is crying. Warfield yells from outside-"Now. Dee, get out of there. NOW."

Josh runs to Nana and hugs her, "I'll be back." Then, he follows Chad out the door. Dee turns in the doorway and looks back at Nana--

"Thank you."

Nana lifts the cup; her hand is shaking. She drops the cup; it clangs to the floor, breaking. Nana leans down to pick it up and cuts her finger. A small drop of blood stains the earthen floor. She raises her eyes, which are pooles of light, and looks into Dee's face--"You're welcome."

Dee glances at the police officer who motions for her to leave. She goes out and catches up with Warfield who is angrily pushing Josh up the drive-way.

"Let go, dad. You're going the wrong way."

"Just keep walking. We'll talk about this when we get home."

"We can go out through the Banyan Tree. It's a'lot closer. Will you just wait--will you listen? Please?"

"There's a snake in that tree. A black mamba. Kill you in twenty minutes." Warfield keeps walking. Faster. Stirring up dust and gravel.

"It's not real."

"That what old witch Easley told you?"

"Her name is Nana Hawkins. She's not a witch."

Dee follows behind, breathing in the dust, trying desperately to catch up with Warfield. "Warfield, Warfield--take Chelsea home. You too, Chad. Josh, we'll go through the Banyan Tree."

"What? Are you nuts? There's a black snake in there."

"Warfield, for once in your life, just go on and let me do this. Take Chelsea home."

Warfield snorts (and it sounds rather like Blitzen's "Are you crazy" snort.) But he follows orders. Amazing. As Chad and Warfield, with Chelsea on his shoulders, disappear down the drive towards the alley, Dee and Josh walk side-by-side through the high grass and the plastic flamingoes. Some of the flowers are opening their blooms and the yard, moonlit and still, seems quite magical. Dee stops, sits down in the soft ferns, catching the dangling roots of the tree. Behind her, the trunk of the tree is smooth and papery, and large enough for a child or a mother to slip through.

"It's a portal, isn't it, Josh? One of those mystical portals that appears every now and then--offering us a glimpse into something bigger and more wonderful than we ever dreamed possible."

Josh, confused, catches hold of one of the roots and swings out. Then, lets his legs hit against the tree trunk. There is a moment of stillness. Josh stares back at the Flamingo Cottage. It seems very quiet. But the Police Officer is still inside. With Nana. Why? He shivers; his mother offers her sweater. He shakes his head, "No". And then he speaks--

"Why were you mean to Nana Hawkins? She took care of us."

Dee holds out her hand; he takes it and sits down on the soft grass, beside her. "Josh, this isn't going to be easy. I hope you're grown-up enough to understand that not everything is as it seems-- as we might hope. Your friend's name is not Nana Hawkins. It's Jane Easley. And she is a patient at Mayfair Manor, a nursing home for elderly persons who are indigent. This property, Flamingo Cottage, was condemned a long time ago by the state. She's trespassing. She takes water from Palm Cottage. And the dogs--they're all stolen. She's not a bad person, Josh . . . she's just old and may be in the beginning stages of . . ."

Josh pulls away. Furious. "I don't believe you. I thought you were different, mom. She doesn't steal the dogs. She rescues them so that they won't be killed. You've got this all wrong. She makes pies so that she can buy presents for poor children whose names are on the paper Christmas Angels and she gets a glass angel--like this one." He reaches into his pocket and takes out the broken angel.

Dee holds the angel in her hands; trying to think, trying to find the right words. "Josh, Miss Easley is very old. She's has a weak heart and she's been missing for almost three months."

"As long as the pies and presents appeared in the Banyan Tree. Don't you see, mom, she isn't crazy. She's just different. She believes in . . . in Life."

"Oh Josh, I've left you alone too much. I've made you grow-up too soon and take responsibility for Chad and Chelsea. Come on, lets' go home. Everything will look much different once we're home and you've had a good night's sleep. Everything always looks different in the morning." She pulls herself up and starts towards a rickety arbor gate to the side of the tree--"Are you sure there's no snake?"

Josh grabs hold of a tree branch and pulls himself up into the tree, disappearing into the vast deep trunk of the tree. Dee turns around. "Josh?"

"This way. Step into the tree."

"Where?"

"Right where you were sitting. It's there. It's kind of a secret door. It's been right here all the time."

Dee walks closer to the tree; she places her hands against the trunk, feeling the energy of the Banyan Tree. Slowly, she slips her foot up, feeling for a hold until she finds an opening. Then, she sees Josh, sitting on a branch that twists and bends just above her.

"Come on. This way, mom."

Dee follows. One step at a time. Slipping through the ferns that grow entwined with the branches. Not seeing exactly where she's going but trusting . . . and listening.

"Mom, she sees what the rest of us miss. All the people most of us just walk by, Nana Hawkins knows their names. She sees-really sees the crazy woman in tennis shoes with a pet bird, or the guy driving the trolley who can sing opera and the greyhound who can barely walk but gives it his all just to finish the race."

He holds out his hand and helps Dee up through the maze of twisted boughs. She follows, listening to her young son--

". . . and she sees the kid nobody notices because he's invisible to everyone else except to someone like her. Someone who sees with her heart."

The greyhounds whimper; their voices rise above the wind, sounding like a cry. A cry for help. Josh and Dee turn and stare back down through the branches at the police officer, leading a calm Nana out of the cottage to a police car. Nana leans down and for a moment, wraps her arms around Whisper. As she does so, she slips a small piece of paper into the dog's collar. The police officer opens the door and Nana climbs inside. He closes her door. Hard. Then walks around to the front of the car, tossing gravel, to frighten the dogs back from the car. Nana presses her face against the window and blows a kiss to the dogs. A second police officer takes a sign out of the car and pounds it into the hard ground. Then, both officers get in the car. The car lights sweep across the yard--illumining the flamingos, the greyhounds and the sign that reads in glaring black letters, "THIS PROPERTY CONDEMNED."

CHAPTER TWENTY-ONE

Sometime in the early hours of half-dreaming, half-waking, just before twilight slips into dawn, Josh wakens. He sits up in bed. Suddenly wide-awake, wondering what sound or distant voice might have stirred him from a restless sleep. He folds his arms behind his head, leans back against his pillow and stares at the ceiling where stars appear, painted on the ceiling. Slowly, the Solar System and then the Milky Way takes shape. Josh closes his eyes to soft eyes ("whisper eyes" as Nana would say)-- "Let's see, the North Pole is probably right about here."

He tosses a small ball up against the ceiling. It bounces back; he catches it. Then, he gets out of bed and walks over to the window. He gazes out over the palm trees at the distant Gulf, dark and silent. Then, slowly, as he looks up at the coming-of-dawn sky, he notices one particular star. Glowing bright, brighter, it seems to illuminate the entire sea of stars until finally it fires a spray of brilliant color and shoots to earth.

"Wow." Josh leans out over the window, hoping to see where the star might have melted into palms or ferns. Then, he glances over his shoulder to see if anyone else is awake. Chad is sleeping soundly; Chelsea, arms wrapped around a stuffed green snake and probably also Baby Ghost, turns restlessly in her sleep. Josh walks over and brushes a strand of loose hair out of her eyes. He sits beside her bed, then, afraid of waking her, goes back to the window.

He stands at the window; then kneels down and stares at the Banyan Tree, solitary, sacred, like an old friend waiting in the shadows. He whispers to the tree, to the stars--and to that Presence that is in both the Banyan Tree and the stars, a secret wish--

"Santa ... I can't believe I'm talking to Santa Claus but just in case you're real, I've got the perfect Mrs. Claus. She loves kids and dogs and she's a great cook. And she's got a heart as big as the North Pole. Bigger."

Chelsea calls out in her sleep for her purse. Josh turns around, sees the plastic pink purse lying on the floor. He reaches it, tosses it next to Chelsea and smiles, "Thank you." And goes back to sleep.

"Anyway, I don't know where she is exactly. And I'm not really sure what her real name is. But you can find her, right? I mean you find anybody. Oh and listen, about Mrs. Upslovsky--that was a mistake."

Suddenly, loud barking rises up from behind the Banyan Tree. Josh pushes the window open wider and stares at a Christmas sleigh drawn by a flying reindeer. It floats over Palm Cottage, circles a row of Christmas Palms and then disappears behind the Banyan Tree.

Josh pulls on a sweatshirt and some jeans, "Wow! Thank you, Santa. Thank you." And about two seconds later, he's climbing out the bedroom window and disappearing through that mystical portal which opens into whatever lies at the back of the Banyan Tree.

CHAPTER TWENTY-TWO

The Flamingo Cottage
That same night

Blitzen flies above the greyhounds, kicking stardust and feathery clouds, gliding, galloping, going in for a graceful landing on the Cottage roof. The sleigh crunches through the shingles and goes a' bit tipsy, so Blitz takes off and settles the sleigh down in an herb garden of sweet lavender, parsley and mint. He has a sprig of the chocolate mint between his teeth before Cape can jump out of the sleigh and trudge up to the house. The greyhounds grow quiet; alert, their noses sniff the air. Then, they sniff the elf. All of them. Cape freezes; he glances back at Blitz but the reindeer is munching parsley and happily nibbling away through the delicious herbs.

"Thanks, Blitz." Cape decides to mimic the trick dog back at the North Pole. He goes down on all fours and holds out his front paw (so to speak), "Stay. Sh-sh . . . Sit. Shake hands. Stay."

The dogs simultaneously cock their heads, lift their tails and their ears and stare at the funny looking elf. Then, curiously, they all sit down on their haunches, hold out their paws and whine. Cape takes this as a very good sign and jumps up, but not too quickly. Then, after shaking paws with each dog, he tosses them a' bit off candy cane and whistles again, "Stay. Stay." The dogs all stay.

Cape makes his way up through the plastic flamingoes and knocks on the cottage door. He catches on that the place is quiet, too quiet. He knocks several times, then peeks through the windows which have been closed, locked tight and one or two have boards across the sills. "H-mm, curious. I don't remember the window being locked." He knocks again, calling out rather cheerfully, "Hello. Hello? Anybody home?"

No answer.

Cape walks around to the side of the Cottage where there are several dog pens--all open. He fills the bowls with fresh water from a large trough, then finds a bag of dog kibble and places a cup of fresh kibble in each dog's bowl. Suddenly, the front screen door mysteriously opens, as if blown open by a strong, warm wind. But there is no wind. The night air is still. Cape glances back at Blitz but the reindeer shakes his head as if to say "Nope, wasn't me." Cape steps inside the Cottage. It's very dark. He tries the light switch; nothing happens and he catches on that there's no electricity. Quietly, whistling a merry Christmas tune to empower his sinking spirits, Cape enters the deserted Cottage.

He manages to pry open one of the windows, letting in a stream of moonlight. The Cottage suddenly seems much cheerier. Cape sees the cup of tea--gives it a sniff, "Ah, Kabusha Tea. Still warm." Then, suddenly, he hears footsteps. Coming from outside. He ducks under the table and waits, still holding the cup of tea.

Josh comes up to the Cottage, through the flowering night bloomers. The dogs greet him with wagging tails. He notices the water in their bowls and the kibble. He whistles for Whisper-- "Hey boy, come here. Where are you?"

From inside the Cottage, actually from underneath the table, comes a distinct whine. And Cape, crunched under the table, feels a wet nose and then a lick from a very wet tongue. The dog Whisper is hiding next to the elf. Cape rises up and knocks his head against the table. "Why are we hiding?" This he whispers to the dog as he slips out from under the table, jumps up onto the kitchen counter and pretends to be working a crossword puzzle.

Josh steps into the cottage. It's shadowy and still. He hears Whisper's tail thumping against the floor. Josh walks towards the sound, knocking over a crate, spilling a thousand crayons. "Hey, boy, take it easy."

The dog comes out from under the table and goes up on all paws, licking Josh's cheeks, his nose, his hands. Josh gives the dog a strong hug. "I miss her, too." He walks over to the window and takes down the glass angel, the one he broke. He doesn't see the elf at first and then, suddenly, he does. Cape slowly lowers the newspaper and gazes over the crossword puzzle at Josh--

"Hello. Very clever. Tenebrae. Your work?"

"Uh-yeah." Josh stares at Cape's ears which are beginning to twitch. "How long, how long have you been there? Why didn't you say something?"

"Oh, I thought I just did. Sorry. Hello, I'm looking for a Nana Hawkins." He jumps off the counter and holds out his hand. He and Josh shake hands. Josh stares into Cape's eyes--bright and wise and burning with a deep wonder. He senses that he has known Cape for a long time. Perhaps, from before he was born. But all he says is--

"Who are you?"

"Caperton Elf. Are you Josh?"

"Yes, how did you …"

"I got, or rather Jingles got your message--you know 'Lovin', Lookin' or Leavin'? Personal ad on the radio show? Pippa? Hello?"

"Yeah, yeah I know. But I didn't e-mail or phone or …"

Josh slips his fingers around Whisper's collar; he's feeling light-headed or rather light-hearted and he's beginning to feel like the room is spinning. Or maybe he's spinning. But he has this absolutely wild, unbelievable idea that Cape might be … he just might be, no that's impossible. He couldn't be …

"I'm an elf. That's right."

"You read my thoughts!"

"Yes, do you think that's magical? It isn't, Josh. You could do it. Actually, you do it all the time. Don't you ever know the phone's going to ring just before it does; or you know who's on the phone even before you pick it up. Or, what about Christmas. Doesn't your mom always know what's on your list … or did you ever think about someone and then there they are. Right smack in front of you?"

"Yeah-maybe. But that still doesn't explain about 'Lovin', Lookin' or Leavin'?"

"Thought form. Yes, it's a tad more complicated. It has to do with energy. When you humans feel something very deeply, really feel it--like when you take a sudden dip in your sleigh and you get this queasy feeling--then, whatever "thought or wish" is connected with that feeling, it has a powerful energy. Energy on a very high level. And it goes out into the universe. And ..."

"Wait, wait -- you lost me."

Cape places his hands over his heart in a gentle gesture; he seems to be thinking. Josh however, is not certain what's going on inside the Flamingo Cottage and he starts backing up. Taking Whisper with him, pulling the dog by his collar. Cape, however, suddenly thinks of a way to explain the "Magic" and slips in between Josh and the door--

"You talked to Santa Claus, right?"

"Yeah, maybe. What do you guys eavesdrop on kids' thoughts. I don't believe in Santa Claus. I was just mad because they took Ms. Hawkins away and left the dogs and it's just not fair. How did you know I talked to Santa Claus?"

Cape keeps his hands folded over his heart and bows, "Josh, Josh, be still. Look at me. All you needed was just a little Belief. Enough belief to get you vibrating on a level high enough for the universe to hear. And you did that. The child deep inside of you must believe, otherwise, we wouldn't have gotten your message. And look, here it is."

Cape unfolds a slip of paper; on it is scrawled in large handwriting--"I've got the perfect Mrs. Santa Claus. She loves kids and dogs and she's a terrific cook. And she's got a heart as big as the North Pole."

Josh stares at the writing, "It's my handwriting. It's my wish. But . . . I don't understand."

"Well, how about a pistachio. Already cracked?" Cape offers a handful of cracked pistachios, palm-flat. "We'll save the big picture for later. Right now, all we've got to do is find this Mrs. Nana Hawkins, right?"

Josh sinks down onto the orange crate; he places his hands over his face and seems about to cry. Whisper licks his face. "It's too late. Nana Hawkins is gone. They took her back to the nursing home."

"Oh really?" Cape starts to sit down on the table, next to Josh. He catches a glimpse of Blitzen, staring at him through the window. "What is it, Blitz?" The reindeer snorts, not once, but twice. Cape gets up and pushes open the window.

Blitz stares at the dog; Whisper stares back at the reindeer. The dog wags his tail. Blitz wags his tail. Blitz blinks. Whisper blinks. "Okay, okay--one of you guys talk."

Blitz shakes his harness; the sound of tinkling bells caresses the soft night breeze. The dog shakes his collar and out falls a slip of newspaper. Cape picks it up; he turns it over and in a corner of the paper sees a yellow star and a name--"Sky Rocket".

"What? What is it?" Josh gets up from the crate and looks at the torn piece of newspaper.

"You tell me. Sounds like some kind of space--maybe something to do with the stars? And there's something else, a number five. Five in the fifth."

Josh suddenly catches on. "What time is it?"

"Early, by the look of the gulls." (He glances out the window and whistles to a seagull.) "Elves don't really think about time. Why?"

"Because I've got to get to Bonita Springs by noon. There's a marked dog in the first race. See, that's what Nana was trying to tell us. Tell whoever happened to find her note. The yellow star means a dog is marked--if he doesn't finish the race, they'll take him out. As in really take him out. And the five is the dog's number. The one is the first race." Josh pushes open the screen door, "Oh, it was nice to meet you."

Cape clears his throat, "Would you like a lift?" He gestures to the sleigh parked under the Banyan Tree. Blitzen paws the grass.

"Wow. Does that thing . . ."

"Fly? Certainly not. But Blitz does. Jump in."

Josh and Cape climb into the sleigh. Blitzen tosses his harness. Bells jingle, jangle and the sleigh rises high up over the Banyan Tree, into a sky tinted the color of a child's finger-drawing of dawn. Lots of purple and streaks of pink and yellow streaming through clouds shaping themselves into giant sandcastles on a vast seascape of blue.

The sleigh follows Gulf Shore drive, dipping in and around well-manicured lawns and "castles" with swimming pooles and sculptures. Blitz nose-dives close to an estate with a playground and two children riding a sea turtle. As he zooms in closer to the sea turtle, the reindeer suddenly kicks out his hooves and does a double-take quick ascent.

"Blitz, old boy, your eyesight's getting to be like Rudolphs. The turtle's a statue. Made of stone."

Josh leans out of the sleigh, staring back down at the beautiful house with its balconies and sculptures and playhouse in the trees. "Hey Cape, did you see the greyhounds. Two of them. Stone statues."

"A sign."

"You think?"

"Absolutely. Nothing appears as coincidence. Blitz, stop being a tourist and fly us to the dog track."

Blitz rises gracefully up above the clouds and head bent low, ears back takes off. Cape rolls his eyes, "May be a' bit bumpy. Hold onto your hat."

"I don't have a hat."

"You do now." Cape sticks the teddy bear top hat on Josh and tosses the reins to Josh, "She's all yours."

Josh sits up, guiding Blitz gently. "Wow, this is incredible."

"It's a wonderful life." Cape pours a couple of hot cocoas and wiggles his nose; whipped cream suddenly appears atop the cocoas. He takes a sip, clicks his fingers and sprinkles the cocoas with sugar.

Not just dull old white sugar, but sugar with pizzazz as in rainbow colored sugar that, when Josh sips his cocoa, adds a touch of cinnamon and a dash of peppermint and even a sneaking suspicion of rich dark chocolate.

Josh licks his lips, "You're really an elf."

"Josh, what do you want for Christmas?"

"Oh, I don't know. Maybe . . . I mean are you asking me, really?"

"Yes."

"A new bike, I guess. A mountain bike."

"What else?"

"That's all. Really. That's enough."

The sleigh runs side by side with a flock of seagulls. There's one gull who is very tired and lagging behind. Blitz calls out something and next thing Josh sees is the gull riding on the back of the reindeer. Hanging on to the harness.

"Yeah, that's Blitz for you. The reindeer's got a good heart. But bossy--" Cape lets out a low whistle. No, now seriously, no joshin' Josh ..." He laughs at his own little elf joke. "What do you really, really want for Christmas?"

Josh is quiet for a long time. He finishes the hot chocolate; puts down the cup and stares at Cape. "I'd like my brother Chad to make one free-shot and for my little sister Chelsea to feel safe enough that she could stop living in a fantasy world. I'd like my dad to stay home once in awhile and maybe take us all out to supper. Or just to the park. I'd like my mom not to be so tired all the time, to lighten up and believe that she's still young and pretty and have some fun. I'd like for us to be a family."

Cape listens. He really listens. And as he listens, a curious thing happens with his ears. They tilt forwards; the tips actually glow as if burning with a white light. "That it?"

Josh sits up straighter, holding onto the reins, talking from his heart which hurts. "No Cape. It isn't. I'd like to live in one house long enough to plant a tree and one day sit in its branches and let the wind blow through my ..."

"Soul." Cape finishes his thought. "Oh, sorry."

Josh smiles, "Yeah, my soul. Thanks. And I'd really, really, really like for Warfield's cell phone to roll over, pack up and move out. What do you want for Christmas, Caperton?"

Cape offers Josh a plate brimming with fruit, blueberries and strawberries, luscious blackberries and tantalizing cheeses with biscuits shaped like elfin hats. Josh takes the plate and hands Cape the reins.

"You know, it's funny, but you're the first child who's ever asked me that." He doesn't miss a beat. "I'd like a telescope."

"Really?"

"Yes, I'd like to see if the children like the toys we bring them. If Christmas touches their lives, their spirits."

"Maybe the reason you've never gotten that telescope, Cape, is because you've never asked."

Cape looks at Josh with a curious light, a knowing in his eyes. But the sleigh dips down, changes course and goes in for a landing.

Below, the dog track rises up like a circus tent. And the parking lot is already steamy and packed with fans. Josh sees Chickee setting up her stand with the umbrellas. He can almost see Emma, perched on her shoulder. And as the sleigh zooms over the entry gates, he catches a glimpse of Nana's friend in the big hat, smiling broadly, selling racing forms. Then, he hears the clanging bell of the trolley and he knows Dominic is down there--singing bass for another choir, bending low and clapping loudly to "Sweet Chariot".

Minutes later, the sleigh touches down behind a row of Royal Palm Trees. And Cape reminds Blitz to "Lie low." Blitz goes down and sticks up his hooves. "Not that low. Just try not to be seen."

Cape and Josh head out across the parking lot. The elf and boy are on a mission and nothing, not rain, or parents or officials with good intentions will turn them from following their destiny.

CHAPTER TWENTY-THREE

Cape and Josh lean out over the railing, at the front of the grandstand section. The greyhounds are parading out onto the track. It's a fast track. Dry and dusty. Josh stares at each dog, then he sees number five--

"There she is. Number five."

"Oh, yes. A' bit scrawny, bless her."

Sky Rocket is a lean, spotted dog with her tail tucked between her hind legs. The muzzle seems too big for her thin, long face. Her bones stick out of her sleek coat.

"She's never going to make it. And without Nana, there's no place safe to take her after the race."

"Then, she'll have to win." Cape winks and takes out the Emerald Bag. "Put your money on it, kid."

"What's in that bag?"

"Lady Luck. Stay here. I'll get us a ticket and give old Lady Luck a pinch on the ..." But his words disappear into the crackling sizzle of the announcer's voice calling out--

"The dogs are in the gate. All except Number Five, Sky Rocket."

Cape takes off; he disappears down through the crowd, climbs up onto the railing and whistles to Sky Rocket. The dog cowers, as if she's been used to being beaten. Cape leans over the railing, throws a handful of the "Sugar and Spice" at the dog who promptly sneezes. Sky Rocket sits back down on her haunches. The dog cocks her head, stares at Cape who tosses more magic dust. Then, the track announcer's voice crackles--

"Here comes Lucky." And the mechanical rabbit shoots out in front of the dogs. The pack of yelping greyhounds race full speed, heads low, paws gliding through sunlight and air. And suddenly, Sky Rocket comes to life. The dog perks up her ears, nose to the ground, and tail high, she flies past the other greyhounds. Actually flies; for her paws never touch the ground. The Track Announcer, stunned, calls the race-- "At the inside turn, it's Gary's Folly followed by Sweet Lilly Rose and . . . no, wait."

Sky Rocket, a gazelle in motion, takes the turn. The announcer bursts out-- "At the far turn, it's . . . I've never seen anything like this. Sky Rocket is taking the lead by one length, two lengths."

Cape joins Josh back up in the grandstand. They stare at the amazing Sky Rocket blistering down the track. And they do a high five. The announcer can hardly believe what's happening--

"Never has there been such a race. Such a dog. Sky Rocket -- from out of nowhere, and I do mean nowhere, has won the race. Amazing. Absolutely incredible. This is truly a Wonder Dog!"

Sky Rocket bounces across the finishing line. With great style.

And Josh and Cape go wild. Cape tosses the Emerald Bag up in the air. It spins, somersaults and out spills the remaining Sugar and Spice on a man, sleeping near the track rail under some old newspapers; the magic dust sprinkles lightly across his bald head. Slowly, he reaches up his fingers, which are gnarled and blistered, and he rises slowly up out of the pile of old papers. He hasn't shaved in years. A cigarette falls limply from parched lips. He coughs. The magic dust on his bald head catches the light and becomes curiously iridescent. Then, slowly, his whole demeanor changes. He begins to chuckle, then belly-laugh. Tears hit his weathered cheeks as he slowly begins to youthen. He blows a kiss to heaven, peeks at his ticket, then disappears into the crowd.

"Oh Christmas, jingles and chocolate kisses!" Cape sighs.

But Josh isn't letting Cape off so easily; he keeps looking at the elf-- "Cape, what exactly did you do?"

"It's kind of hard to explain. The Magic dust gives you your heart's desire." Cape walks over and picks up the empty bag; he turns it inside out and right side in. It is quite empty. Not a sprinkle left. Not even a breath of a wish left. Nothing. "Well, looks like from here on out, Josh, we're on our own."

"Well, at least we're rich." Josh points to the Board where the winning amounts are drawing quite a strong, if stunned, reaction from the bewildered crowd.

Cape pulls his spectacles down off the top of his head and tries to read the numbers, "Oh, I can't quite read that. Need to boost up on my carrot-tomato juice. Too much cocoa."

"Well, Caperton Elf, the Superfecta pays "$100,000. Got a comb?"

"Is it my ears?" Cape blushes.

"No, your hair. The IRS is goin' want to take your picture."

CHAPTER TWENTY-FOUR

Big Sam counts out the cash, grinning broadly. He clucks his tongue, eyeing the boy and small man standing on the opposite side of the cashier's window. "So, you and the elf got lucky, eh?"

Cape goes up on tip-toe, whispering, "How did you know I'm an elf?"

"How could I not know? Wait here." Sam disappears behind the window. There's the sound of a dog's tail thumping and suddenly, from behind the counter, ears appear. Followed by a spotted face and warm eyes. The old greyhound sniffs Josh's open hand.

"Josh, I'm running a little short on time here. Any idea where Nana might be?"

"Oh sure. Thanks for saving Sky Rocket. I know Ms. Hawkins will really appreciate . . ."

"Yes, but where is she?"

"A nursing home. Mayfair Manor." The dog jumps down as Sam comes back from around the window.

"Right."

Suddenly, Josh turns and takes off, calling over his shoulder--

"Cape, oh man, I forgot something. The Christmas Angel. The tree, They light it tonight."

"But where will we find you?" Cape can't follow because Big Sam is counting out more and more bills. The stack of bills is almost as tall as the little guy. "Josh?"

Josh is on the escalator, going down. Just before he slips out of sight, he waves to Cape, "I'll leave a note with the angel." Then, he's gone. And Sam is holding a camera right smack dab in front of the little elf's face. There's a loud hissing noise. A click. A wink. And bright white light hits Cape.

"Say Merry Christmas, Sam." Sam grins and readies the camera. Suddenly, a tall, handsome man with thick hair pops his face into the picture and grins, waving his winning ticket. The stranger with the ticket grins, "Merry Christmas Sam."

Cape glances at the stranger, "Do I know you?"

The stranger shakes his beautiful thick hair and "Magic dust" fills the air. Cape sneezes. Just as Big Sam clicks another shot. Zing.

Cape and the lucky stranger are caught forever in a black and white photograph--Elf and the guy who will spend the rest of his life talking about how a little white sugar spilled from heaven onto his ticket, his head and his heart. And the rest was all "Sugar and Spice and Everything (and he means everything) NICE!"

CHAPTER TWENTY-FIVE

Josh gazes up at the Christmas Tree near the fountain in historic Old Naples. There's not a breath of air stirring. The streets are silent. Tony's Off Third, with its delicious flourless chocolate cake, éclairs with real whipped cream and key lime pie, has closed for the night. As are all the other shops--the bookstore, Sassy Fox, even the Beach House with windows of mannequins in bathing suits. Third Street waits in breathless anticipation of Christmas.

Josh ties the Emerald Bag, bulging with dollar bills, onto a tree branch. He slips a note in the bag and starts to walk away. But the wind is playing tricks; blowing sweet and warm across the towering pine tree. And then, the tree glistens. Every light on the tree suddenly burns brightly. And the star at the tip-top glows with iridescence so brilliant that even Josh turns, facing this strange and wonderful Wind.

Awed by the presence of something unseen, something powerful and wonderful in that Wind.

And it is in that moment that Josh decides what he must do. He reaches up on tip-toe for the bag; and quickly writes something on the piece of paper. Then, he whistles. Two long whistles and two short. From out of the shadows, there's the sound of footsteps and Whisper steps into the glow of a streetlamp. The dog also feels the wind, ruffling his coat. Then, a curious thing happens. From out of the streetlamps, all along Third Avenue, snow begins to fall.

And it is still falling by the time Josh rides his bike (with Whisper trailing behind). . . past the Lilly Shop, and the Pub—and leaving behind a brilliantly lighted Christmas Tree, sprinkled with SNOW.

CHAPTER TWENTY-SIX

Outside The Sweet Bay Magnolias Residential Care Home, a pouting stone frog pours water into a fountain that dried up years ago. A lizard basks lazily in the dappled light, then disappears into the cracked basin. Sweet Bay Magnolias, once a grand old lady on the north side of Naples, is quietly disappearing into tall licorice grass and windblown thistle gone to seed.

There's not a Sweet Bay Magnolia anywhere in sight.

Cape, in sunglasses and a cap that says "Royal Poinsettia", comes out of the main entrance of the Magnolias sipping a Super-sized Frosty Root Beer. He takes the steps two at a time. Nana follows, completely amazed at the adeptness, the agility and the charm of the dashing stranger who has just rescued her from "Pinochle at Seven" and "Hot Milk Before Bed at eight." She laughs out loud, causing Caperton to pause and turn around.

"Did I say something wrong?"

"No. No! I was just remembering the look on that dear woman's face when you told her you loved the oatmeal raisin cookie that her granddaughter left for Santa last Christmas."

"Delicious. Light on the raisins and heavy on the cinnamon."

"But what on earth did you tell those people that made them change their minds?"

Cape hesitates, offers his hand to Nana and guides her across the parking lot to the sleigh. "The truth, Ms. Hawkins?"

She stares at the sleigh, then at the reindeer, then at Cape and her eyes burn glitter with girlish delight, "Please."

"Well, I reminded Dr. Stewart that the reason he never got that chemistry set was because he kept wetting the bed and I told Dr. Morris that the reason she never got the rocking unicorn was because she never learned to share her toys and that nurse, well, she's the naughty girl with the curl and I don't have to tell you that when she's good she's very, very good but when she's bad . . . Ah, here we go."

He offers her his hand, bowing slightly. Nana climbs into the sleigh. Loving every single second of the adventure. She laughs--

"And they let me go, just like that?"

"Well, not quite." He climbs in beside her and takes the reins. "I had to promise The Magnolias a new west wing and a sleigh full of toys. Shall we?"

"Oh Mr. Elf, you are clever."

Blitzen snorts, takes off and the sleigh rises above the tree tops.

"Oh, by the way. My name is Caperton Elf. You may call me Cape. Everyone at the North Pole does. Jingles and . . . Whoa."

Blitzen takes a sudden detour around a storm cloud. Thunder ripples across the sky. And Nana takes one quick look back down as the Magnolias disappear into a sea of clouds. The sleigh hits some rather stormy weather; Cape shoots up an umbrella and Nana scoots over closer to the elf. And before the sleigh somersaults into high gear, heading straight for the Gulf, Nana and Cape are good friends. After all, they're kindred spirits. Believers who see with their hearts. And between such souls, there lies a depth of friendship even before the first secret is shared.

By the time they reach Old Naples, the sky has made good its promise of rain. Large drops fall against Cape's umbrella; he and Nana skip over puddles, making a path up Third straight for the Christmas tree. The fountain splashes water over a band of cherubs, stone of course, holding trumpets to their lips. The lights are no longer lit and the rain suddenly stops.

Nana and Cape come up the steps, and suddenly stop. A young woman, Dee, sits beside the fountain. She has her head bent down, as if praying. Cape glances at Nana who reaches out a hand to touch the young woman on the shoulder--

"Are you all right, dear?"

Dee looks up. She's been crying, "Yes, oh, I . . ."

"Goodness, honey, here." Nana hands Dee a tissue. "Blow your nose."

"They let you go!"

"Well, yes. Thanks to Mr. Caperton Elf. And you're Josh's mother. May I sit down?"

"Please. It's a little wet." Dee scoots over and makes room for Nana next to her beside the fountain. Cape holds the umbrella over the heads of both Nana and Dee and pretends not to eavesdrop. But his ears are beginning to twitch.

"My compliments, honey. You have raised three beautiful, sensitive and loving children. That's not an easy thing in today's world."

Dee starts to cry again. Nana hands her another tissue. Then another. Cape steadies the umbrella and ducks underneath. "And lucky, I might add. Josh, ya know, picked a Superfecta." He winks.

But Dee starts to cry again. Her nose turns red and she is so distraught that Cape feels like he's going to cry. Nana keeps handing out tissues, saying "Dear, dear, it can't be as bad as all that. What's the matter? Tell us after you've had a chance to blow your nose."

Cape blows his nose. Rather loudly.

"Josh is missing. I've looked everywhere. He was so disappointed-- he said we didn't understand you, that we didn't give you a chance, Nana--may I call you Nana?"

"Please do."

"And you know what, Josh was right. I knew you were a kind sweet old lady right from the minute I saw you telling stories to the children. Not that you're old-- but, oh you know what I mean .. well, I think I was jealous. I never have time to tell the children stories. I'm always so busy doing the laundry or cleaning the house or chasing after Warfield's socks. And that's another thing, I never stand up to Warfield. He . . . he's always on his cell phone. And now, I think, Josh may have run-away. That he's gone somewhere, trying to find you, trying to rescue you, Nana, the way you rescued him. But he . . . he's just a little boy. And anything could happen!"

"You're frightened, dear. Let go of that fear. It has a very low energy and it'll attract things of the same energy. Now, lets' think of something . . . something wonderful."

Cape stares at Nana. Absolutely enthralled. Delighted. "How on earth--you know about energy? About "ah-ah"?"

Dee stares back and forth between the elf and Nana. Trying to make sense of what is nonsense.

"Of course. I've done the "ah-ahs" with great feeling ever since I was a child. My father took me with him on his travels to the Far East; he was quite fascinated with the Suffis and . . ."

"Do you know where Josh is?" Dee suddenly stands up, knocking the umbrella out of Cape's grasp. It rolls around, sideways, upside down, then magically turns right-side up and goes airborne until it is once again over Nana's head. Dee shakes her head, "Nana? Mr. Elf? Do either of you . . ."

"Not exactly. But, he's been here." Cape reaches up on tip-tip-toe and takes down the Emerald Bag; he hands the note to Nana who reads it aloud--

"Tennebrae. Shadows before dawn." Nana smiles. "Yes, of course." Nana slips the Emerald Bag back on the tree, next to a paper angel shaped to look like a greyhound. A sudden strong gust of wind whips across the fountain and the tree lights up.

Dee stares up, amazed--"How did that happen?"

"Magic!" He winks at Nana. "Now if you two ladies would be so kind--there's a sleigh and reindeer waiting for us, just beyond that Pub."

Cape holds out an arm to Dee, and the other to Nana and they take off across Third Street toward the Pub. As they walk under the streetlight, snow sprinkles down. Dee catches some in her hands, makes a snowball and places it in her pocket.

"You think it will last?" Cape asks rather matter-of-factly.

"For the rest of my life." Dee winks and as they near the Pub, Blitz comes out from behind an alley, wearing mistletoe in his antlers and chewing a big, really big pickle. Blitz reaches for the pickle--"Blitz, you're going to have to stay out of the Pub. You and your pickles."

The reindeer goes down on his two front legs in a graceful bow to Dee and Nana; he gives his harness bell a shake and rolls his eyes at Blitz and the snort sounds something like, "Mistletoe or pistachios-- what's the difference?"

Seconds later, Nana and Dee are enjoying a handful of cracked pistachios, gazing down over the Christmas Tree as the sleigh climbs silently. Higher and higher. Heading straight towards the abandoned amusement park.

CHAPTER TWENTY-SEVEN

Josh and the greyhounds, all of the greyhounds, wait in the shadows of the lemon trees. A strong, eerie wind blows back the leaves of the trees. Branches creak beneath the steady pounding of rain. Whisper licks Josh's face, his hands.

"It's all right. She'll come. I know she will. We just have to wait."

The wind blows hard, stirring old memories. Josh gazes up at the looming Ferris Wheel. Rusted, paint peeling, it turns slowly, round and round. The empty seats move back and forth, as if phantom children played up there, on the thin metal rims. Waiting. Watching for run-away children. Taunting them to come up to the top--up where the wind is strong, and fly.

Josh closes his eyes. He wraps his jacket around Whisper who is shaking and seems very, very cold. The dogs huddle around Josh, frightened, not understanding why they have come to this deserted place. Then, the greyhounds whine and the low whine changes into a growl. Frightened, Josh stands, stepping out from the lemon tree into the open. Rain hits his face. For a moment, he can't see. And then, he catches on. The bright lights coming from the ferns--they are eyes. The eyes of a wild creature. Josh holds his breath; his heart is pounding. He calls to Whisper to "stay back."

The eyes come closer. And Josh leans down and breaks off a branch from the tree; he moves in closer to the animal. There is a terrible moment in which Josh is consumed by fear. And the only way out is to keep going--deeper into the ferns, deeper into the labyrinth of shadows and eerie sounds. Then, the footsteps stop.

And Josh stands still. Staring at a small brown animal, also staring at him.

"You're a snipe."

The animal goes up on its hind legs. It is as if the snipe wants to make certain that Josh sees him. Josh puts down the stick, and holds out his hand to the snipe, "You really are . . ."

A voice calls out cheerfully, "So, you brought the greyhounds."

Cape pushes back the branches of a gnarled old lemon tree and steps into a pool of moonlight. Josh turns and almost runs straight into his friend's arms, "Cape, hey, man, I mean elf, I'm glad to see you."

"You miss me. I turn up. That's how elves are."

"I was beginning to see things."

"See things?"

"It doesn't matter. Yeah, I had to bring the dogs. They were going to send them to the Humane Society. My mom will think I'm crazy but . . ."

Dee, walking beside Nana, comes from out of the shadows, holding out her arms to Josh. "Well, some moms might think one neurotic hamster, a rabbit, a lizard, parakeet and a dog . . . one princess, one imaginary Baby Ghost, one basketball star, a hyper husband and a very wise son might be enough for one family, but actually, I think one more--two more--a dozen more greyhounds are just what this family needs to take root."

"Thanks, mom." Then, he finally hears what she's just said and he runs straight towards her. "You mean it? About 'taking root'. We're not moving?"

"Nope, unless well, maybe across the street. There's an Old Flamingo Cottage on the back side of that Banyan Tree--just went on the market."

"What about the San Diego Wal-Mart?"

"There's a Wal-mart here. And anyway, your dad's phones disappeared. All of them. It's like they just packed up and took off. Josh, did you know that the Old Banyan Tree has a secret stairway inside, and the walls of the tree shine from all the children who have played deep in its secret tunnels and rooms. There's even a room wide enough for a mother and her son to sit and talk and catch-up on the last oh, say ten years of his life. What do you say? Shall we explore the Banyan Tree?"

Josh gives his mother a hug. A really tight hug; then he catches a glimpse of Nana, standing silently behind Dee. Waiting. "You two met?"

"Your mother and I had a lovely chat in the sleigh flying over here."

Josh glances back at Cape—"So, uh, Cape, you met Ms. Hawkins? What do you think?"

"I think Santa is going to love this surprise. And speaking of the Big Elf, it's almost Christmas Eve. We haven't much time, Josh."

Josh feels a sudden deep pain, sharper and more real than any pain he has ever felt before. "So, this is it? Good-bye?"

Cape's ears twitch. "Not good-bye, Josh. 'Merry Christmas'."

Josh leans in close to Cape and hugs him, "Merry Christmas, Cape." He whispers, "Watch those ears."

Cape smiles at Dee, "I'll have a shiny new train under that tree next year."

"A train? Oh no, another boy?" Dee laughs and folds her arms around Josh as they wave good-bye.

"No" it's Cape's turn to grin, "There'll be a baby doll, too."

"No, Cape--you don't mean, twins?"

Cape laughs, "You have a wonderful family! Blessings." Cape folds his hands over his heart in a solemn gesture and bows.

Josh steps forward, "What's that mean, Cape?"

"It means, 'The god in me, salutes the god in you.' Then, Cape steps back and bows again. And this time, Josh places his hands over his heart and meets the elves' eyes which are beaming strength and love and something deeper, a joy that goes out from Cape's heart to Josh's heart, connecting the very essences of their being forever.

Nana gives a hug to each greyhound, and gratefully looks at Dee and Josh, "Thank you. Take good care of our greyhounds, Josh."

"It's a promise, Ms. Hawkins."

Dee puts her arm around Whisper; then, the greyhounds, Dee and Josh all step back and watch as Cape holds out his arm to Nana and leads her over to the Christmas sleigh. He steps back, does a slight bow, "Ms. Hawkins--"

"Please, call me Nana."

"Nana, do you like adventures?"

"Oh, I love adventures." She is about to sit down when Whisper breaks free and bounds up and into her lap. "Oh, oh dear. Mr. Elf, would it be all right if Whisper . . ."

"I don't see why not. She might even get to be lead reindeer."

The old greyhound licks Cape's face and shivers. Blitzen rolls his eyes. And suddenly, the Christmas Sleigh rises up through the branches of the lemon trees, higher than the Ferris Wheel, straight towards a sea of stars.

Cape leans back and slackens the reins, "Nana, there's someone I want you to meet. A jolly old elf . . ."

"Oh, I just love elves. Is it anyone I know?"

"Could be you've known him a very, very long time."

As the Christmas sleigh rises up through the rain, Cape stares at the palms of his hands, breathing deeply. A sizzling white light shoots out from his hands--straight towards the storm clouds. And suddenly, the wind changes direction and the palm trees below toss and turn, blowing in a completely opposite direction. The thunder storm changes into a mystical snow storm. And as the sleigh disappears into the falling snowflakes, Nana whispers to the greyhound-- "I wonder if he likes lemon pie with red and green meringue?"

CHAPTER TWENTY-EIGHT

PRESENT TIME
NORTH POLE

Cape gazes at the stars. There's the sound of footsteps, coming up the path. He turns and sees Santa Claus coming towards him. He's whistling and sounding like a very jolly elf.

"Caperton, I thought I might find you up here. Great view of the stars. You can see the whole Milky Way. Might even catch a few shooting stars--not just from the Mrs., of course." He chuckles and his belly shakes.

"Good evening, sir. You seem in good spirits." Cape starts to stand but Santa sits down beside him. Santa glances at the crystal angel--

"A present from a child?"

"Yes sir, if he had different ears, he could be an elf."

"May I?"

Cape holds out the angel. Santa takes it, turns it over in his hands. Notices that the wing has been glued back on. "Thank goodness for superglue. Saves a' lot of tears on Christmas morning."

"It's for Mrs. Claus."

"Oh, I see. You know, Caperton, elves come in all shapes and sizes, but they carry the spirit of Christmas in their hearts. Here, before I forget, this was in the back of the sleigh. I think you've waited quite a long time for this present."

164

Cape takes the present; it's wrapped in Christmas paper--with elves. Santa brushes the snow off his pants, gives his suspenders a little boost and jumps to his feet.

"You know, Cape, I'm so much more flexible than I used to be.

"Why is that, sir?"

"Well, I got Yoga Barbie to talk Jingles into going for something less bouncy. I like yoga. I also like creamy yogurt with chocolate sauce. Think I'll have a little treat before I pack."

"Oh, so you're going to pack."

"Merry Christmas, Cape."

"Merry Christmas, Santa. Oh and give my best to Mrs. Claus and Lollipop."

"Dag-gone greyhound wants Rudolph's job." Santa laughs and takes off jogging back down the path. Cape watches him, then sits back down and unwraps the present. A telescope falls out onto Cape's lap. Attached to the telescope is a note, "Merry Christmas, Cape. Josh."

Cape holds the telescope up to his eyes and tries to gaze out past the stars, searching for a Cottage behind a Banyan Tree and a boy . . . but his eyes can't see, for he's crying. So, he places the telescope down and folds his hands across his heart. Then he whispers to a shooting star, "Thank you, Josh. You're more elf than you know. 'The god in me salutes the god in you. Forever."

The star shapes itself into the face of a Child. A child with light green eyes and glasses too big for his small nose, so they keep slipping down . . . A Child who sees with his heart. Who is also gazing up at the stars from his loft room in a recently restored Cottage. Behind the Banyan Tree. And downstairs, his family--his dad and mom, his brother and sister and twin baby brother and sister gather beneath the Christmas Tree. Josh too sees the shooting star and just before he slips downstairs to join his family, he folds his hands over his heart and whispers, "The god in me salutes the god in you, Cape. Forever."

CHAPTER TWENTY-NINE

On a tropical paradise somewhere south of the North Pole, a lovely lady in a broad-brimmed straw hat, and dark sunglasses places a tiny sand sculpture of a miniature sleigh drawn by eight reindeer and one greyhound on top of a sandcastle. A wave tickles her bare toes and sneaks up closer to the castle moat. Then, a shadow falls across the turrets and a man's voice catches her by surprise-

"Missed me?"

She turns around and stares at Santa Claus, dressed in Christmas drawers with a snorkel and a sand bucket. She laughs, "Not a' bit."

He gently kisses the top of her sunbonnet and as she loosens the ties on her straw hat, she seems to grow much younger. There is a light about her. A lightness about her being that speaks of a deep peace within her loving spirit. She looks into his face, and smiles, "Merry Christmas, Santa."

"Merry Christmas, Mrs. Claus."

They walk hand-in-hand towards the Gulf; and behind them, from a boom-box by the sandcastle, Pippa's voice rises above the crashing waves, "Cuddly. Cute as a bunny. 5'8'. Big ears. Soft tail. Loves to hop and hide eggs. No dogs.' Wait a minute. Wait just a minute.' Giggles burst in on the personal ad. "No, this can't be. The Easter Rabbit is looking for a wife?"

Seagulls honk noisily. The waves rise and crest, white-capped and sunlit. And as the sun, a fiery red ball disappears into the Gulf, a solitary star appears low on the horizon. Then Pippa's voice whispers, "For 'Lovin', Lookin' or Leavin', I'm Pippa. Wishing you the love of your life."

The star magically becomes a shooting star, trailing a rainbow that shapes the words, "Happy New Year" across the sky.

And the rest, dear sweet Caite, is destiny.

> Much love,
> Mrs. Santa Claus

ABOUT THE AUTHOR

Attorney turned author, Margaret Price comes to the literary arena inspired by true-life stories gathered while traveling Kentucky's backroads as director of the Kentucky Oral History Project. Price is an Honors graduate from Northwestern University and the U.K. College of Law where she served on the Law Journal editorial staff. Price's commitment to children's advocacy speaks through her creative works—including her screenplays, CARR CREEK (optioned by Alex Rose Productions), the award-winning LOOKING FOR MRS. SANTA CLAUS (produced in San Francisco), DOVE & DANDELION (Honors, Louisville's Film Festival) and UNGENTLE TRUTH,(winner Minneapolis Screenlabs.) Her published stories appear in the Chocolate series (Simon & Schuster). Presently teaching Screenwriting at U.K., Price lives in Lexington with her husband, Gary Swim and their three daughters, Meredith, Julie and Katie.

Looking For Mrs. Santa Claus

Printed in the United States
38276LVS00003B/206